BATTERIES NOT INCLUDED

Tony McFadden

Copyright © 2021 Tony McFadden

All rights reserved.

ISBN:978-0-6485628-4-9

DEDICATION

Thanks to all of the frontline support workers, working their ever-loving arses off in absolutely frustrating circumstances

.

You know who you are.

DISCLAIMER

All characters in this book are fictitious. Any resemblance to real people is entirely coincidental.

This book is set in Australia, and written in Australia. It has Australian sayings and spellings.

And swearing. A decent amount of swearing.

You have been warned.

ACKNOWLEDGMENTS

The journey I've followed over the past slightly more than a decade is on the back of the feedback I get from you, my readers.

Thank you so much.

Even the crap reviews help me.

PROLOGUE

Andy Goh loved sunrise more than any other time of day. It was his quiet time, alone with his thoughts, and his coffee, the cool of the night slowly burning off with the rising sun. He stood at the kitchen sink window in his robe, looking down over his pool and beyond that to his small jetty poking into Sydney Harbour. Small, but large enough for his sailboat, a 15-metre catamaran he took out maybe four times a year, if he was lucky. The Manly Ferry cut through the water, right to left, heading for Circular Quay, leaving a wake behind it glittering in the early morning sun.

He cupped the mug of black coffee and sighed. Life had been good to him. A lot of hard work, to be sure, but what was it they said? Find something you enjoy, and you'll never have to work a day in your life. They should also have said to make sure you hire smart people to do the parts of your job you dislike or were poor at. It took him a year to figure that out. And almost a decade to be really comfortable moving accountability down the corporate ladder to the people who actually did the work.

He checked the time. It was 6:35. He had a breakfast meeting. A meeting with a guy about a problem he needed solved, one he knew he couldn't solve on his own. The references checked out. And if the results were satisfactory, maybe he'd bring them on permanently. He recognised his company was weak with data and financial governance. He needed a new set of eyes.

He checked the time again. The morning newspaper should have been tossed over his fence by now.

He put his cup on the counter and padded barefoot out the front door. Even though it was only weeks away from winter, Australia was going through a warm patch. The flagstone on his front step was already starting to warm in the early sun. He smiled. The paper, rolled and held by an elastic band, was in the middle of his driveway. The kid had a good arm. He stepped off the front stairs and walked over the terra cotta tile under the portico at the entrance. The paper was a good 15 metres this side of the gate.

He stopped and frowned.

The gate was partially open. It was a very sturdy gate, opening from the side, run on rails, large wheels on a track operated by a motor which only engaged if the proper code was entered from the outside or a concealed button pushed from the inside. No joins in the middle. No weaknesses.

And he was supposed to have security manning the gate.

He looked around for his head of security. "Hey, Mike." He took a couple of steps toward the gate. "Mike, what the hell is the gate doing open?"

He took another couple of steps around the corner of the house and noticed the smoke billowing up from the far side of the wall. A flame licked close to the gum tree on his side of the wall. "Shit."

He sensed the person behind him just before something hard smashed down at the base of his skull.

Everything went black as his face hit the tiles.

CHAPTER ONE

Nick Harding pulled his car to the kerb just around the corner from his destination and checked his teeth and poorly tied tie in his visor mirror. His scalp was shiny, freshly shaved that morning and carefully lotioned. He adjusted his tie a tweak and flipped the visor up. The car was almost fifteen years old. It had over 300,000 km on the clock. The paint was dull from years of Australian sun and the windscreen pitted. His car stood out in this neighbourhood, and he hated it for that. He scowled. Around the corner was the front gate to Andy Goh's house. Andy Goh's three storey, with a pool, ocean front and 2400 square metres of land, house on Sydney Harbour. Why Andy wanted to hire him was a mystery.

Goh's wealth came from his introduction of a fully Australian-made electric vehicle to the market, grabbing a significant portion of the EV pie. The brand competed well internationally. The market was barely tapped. A self-made billionaire. Not one of these losers who inherited their wealth.

And for some inexplicable reason he wanted to meet with a PI who had barely $1000 in the bank, significant periods of time between cases and a burgeoning drinking problem.

Nick grunted and pulled from the kerb. The curiosity was killing him. He accelerated around the corner and slammed on the brakes, stopping in the middle of the road. The wrought-iron fence around Goh's property stretched on his left forward along the street to the gate.

Two marked police cars, lights still strobing, were pulled up by the open gate. An unmarked car with red and blue lights flashing in the grill and an ambulance were further in, by the front door of the palatial house. Beyond the gate, thin tendrils of smoke wafted off the burnt-out shell of a vintage Volkswagen Beetle.

He pulled to the kerb and turned off the engine. Stared for a second at the uniform leaning on the wall by the open gate, then got out.

He straightened his suit, sucked in his stomach and tried for a nonchalant, yet confident look. He took a deep breath and walked toward the young cop.

He smiled and nodded. "Hey, mate. What's going on here?"

The constable righted himself and adjusted his belt. He held out a hand, palm forward, stopping him. "This is an active crime scene, sir. I'll have to ask you to stand back."

Nick took his identification, a laminated Commercial and Private Inquiry Agent card, out of his inside suit pocket. He flipped open the wallet and showed it to the cop. "Nick Harding. Private Investigator." He handed him a business card and folded the ID back in his pocket and pointed generally into the drive. "I've got an appointment. In here. What's the crime? Was Andy Goh robbed?"

"An appointment?"

Nick nodded. "An 8:30 breakfast meeting."

"With?"

"The big guy. Goh."

The constable pulled a small notepad from his breast pocket and clicked a pen to life. "When was this appointment arranged?"

"Last night."

"What time did you talk to him?"

Nick shook his head. "It was by email. He said he wanted to engage me for something, but wasn't specific." He took a step toward the gate. "The guy's a billionaire. I don't want to keep him waiting. Okay if I go in?"

"What time was the email sent?"

"A little after 7:30. Like I said, last night. Look, I'm a stickler for promptness. And I'm sure he is, too."

"No hurry, mate. You're not keeping him waiting." The constable flipped his notebook closed. "Someone beat him to death when he stepped out to pick up his newspaper this morning. Around 6:40, 6:45."

Nick took a step back. "Really? Seriously?"

"Yeah."

"He seriously got a newspaper, a *paper* newspaper, delivered? A tech guy like him?" He shook his head, surprised. "Really?"

The constable shrugged. "He's dead. Meeting's cancelled."

"Shit." Nick scratched his jaw. "Okay if I check it out? I'm, ah, sort of involved in this."

The constable leaned back and looked through the gate at the crime scene and shrugged. "We're pretty much finished up. Stay outside of any tape."

Nick watched a couple of people in bunny suits slide a body bag into the back of the coroner's wagon. "Not a problem. Thanks."

The constable smiled and leaned back against his car. "Watch where you step. Good luck."

He walked through the gate and over the very well-maintained drive that arced a long sweeping curve to the left toward a portico at the front of the three-storey home. Halfway to the front door a small, wiry man intercepted him and poked him in the chest with his index finger.

"Stop."

Nick looked down at the index finger, considering it. "I was invited." He continued looking at the finger. "You want to stop doing that?" He returned his gaze to his assailant. "Who are you?"

"Mike Murphy. Mr Murphy to you. I run security for Mr Goh." He had the remnants of a Belfast accent. He pushed gently on Nick's sternum. "Leave."

"Not going to fight you. But I really was invited. Nick Harding. PI." He slowly reached inside his suit and extracted his ID. "Would you know why Andy wanted to meet?"

"It's *Mr* Goh to you." Mike inspected the ID, then handed it back. "And I've never heard of you. He would have informed me if he was looking for a PI." He crossed his arms. "I and my team do all of his investigations. No need to go outside the family."

"You don't look like family." He rubbed his sternum. "I think you left a bruise."

"Suck it up. We're all one big happy family here."

"Can't be that happy if he went outside the," Nick held up quote fingers, "'family' to hire me." He looked over Murphy's head at the front door. A tall woman watched them with a cup of coffee in one hand and her mobile phone in the other. "Is that the Mrs Goh?"

Mike looked over his shoulder. She waved him over. "Wait here."

Nick watched the little man jog to the front door. A row of low hedges curving with the drive obscured their feet, but he could tell from her posture she wasn't in heels. The differences between the two was sharp. He was short, hard-edged and pasty white. She was a head-and-a-half taller, elegant and chocolate. She wore faded denim trousers and a peach golf shirt, her hair in a ponytail. The two had an animated discussion for a couple of minutes and it was very apparent who the boss was. She glared and Mike shook his head in resignation, then waved Nick to join them.

He took a deferential step back as Nick approached.

"I'm Nick Harding." He held out his hand for the woman. "I'm very sorry to hear about your husband."

She slipped her mobile in her back pocket and shook his hand. "Kirra. Thank you. Why are you here? Murphy says Andy hired you?"

Nick shrugged. "Not yet. That's what the meeting this morning was to discuss. I guess that's not going to happen now. Sorry to take your time." Nicked looked at the doorbell camera and the camera at the top of the portico. "I think you've got it all covered, though." He turned to leave.

Kirra touched Nick's arm. "Hang on a second. Come in for coffee, at least." She nodded at Mike. "I'm good. Go back to whatever it was you were supposed to be doing."

Mike glared at Nick. They both watched him walk around the back of the house, then Kirra stood aside and let Nick enter.

The foyer was two stories high, with a white marble floor. Stairs at the far end curled to an upper floor. Three steps down on the left led to a large living area, a fireplace on the far wall. Black leather furniture accented the white marble floor and walls. Aboriginal art hung on the walls. The house was an example of understated elegance.

"Nice place, Mrs Goh."

"Kirra. And I go by my family name. Kirra Roach. Can I get you something to drink? Coffee? Tea? Whiskey?"

Nick smiled. "Coffee, black, is fine. A little early for whiskey, I think."

"Figured you were one of those hard-boiled Private Eyes I'm always hearing about. Heavy drinking, hard living." She eased into a chair and sat sideways; her legs dangled over the arm of the chair. "Coffee will be out here shortly. Why did my husband hire you?"

Nick sat in the sofa across from her. A glass and chrome coffee table sat between them. "Like I said, he hasn't. Didn't. That's what this meeting was supposed to be for. You don't know?"

"He mentioned something about money missing from the company. Quite a lot, if I understood. But other than that, nothing. Can I hire you to find out who killed him?"

"You don't seem too distraught."

"I'm serious. I'd like to hire you. What are your rates?"

A young man came in with two cups of coffee and placed the tray on the coffee table and backed out.

"I'm sure the police will have the perps picked up before I finish this coffee. Saw the cameras out front. Plus that security guy, what's is name, Mike, seems pretty competent."

"Yeah, no. Murphy checked the footage. Nothing's been recorded since midnight. He thinks there was a power bump or something." She shook her head. "And I slept late. I flew back from America and didn't get home until after midnight." She let out a deep breath. "I'm sure the police will work this case hard. The media is going to be all over it."

Nick sat back. "Hey, yeah. No press outside. How in the hell did you manage that?"

"Pink is touring. They're all following her. Lucky us." She leaned forward and picked up her coffee. "Work for me?"

Nick sipped his coffee and looked around the room. There was more money tied up in furniture than he figured he made in his life. He took the coffee and walked to one of the paintings. Waves of white dots through a sea of multicoloured blue dots. He pointed at it. "Nice. How much did this one cost?"

"Impolite question. A shade over thirty-seven dollars and six weeks."

Nick smiled. "You painted this? Very nice. I thought canvas cost more than that."

"I buy in bulk. You haven't answered me."

Nick handed his coffee cup to Kirra. "I won't deny that I could use the money, but I make a point of not getting in the way of professional law enforcement. Our dislike is mutual. Thanks for the coffee. It's better than anything I make. I'm sorry for your loss. I'll show myself out."

A cleaning crew was finishing up outside a few metres from the portico. Nick looked at the angle from the cameras to the crime scene. Clear shot. There should have been footage. It could have been wrapped up before noon. "Shit luck."

He stood at the gate and looked back toward the crime scene. The hedges blocked the view. "Perfect."

The young constable stood by his shoulder. "What is?"

Nick turned. "You're still here? It's pretty much wrapped up here, mate." He held up a forefinger. "Hang on. You worked the graveyard, didn't you? Grabbing as much overtime as you can. Got it." He clapped him on the shoulder. "My tax dollars barely at work. Well done. Catch you later."

Mike walked through the house looking for Kirra, finding her in the lower pool room. Snooker, not chlorinated water. She was rolling a snooker ball across the green felt surface, watching it bank gently off the cushions, missing a pocket every time.

She looked up as he walked in. "What in the hell happened, Mike?"

He shook his head. "Still trying to figure it out. We should head into the station to give them statements. Get it out of the way."

She rolled a ball with extra force, hitting the cushion and bouncing off the slate and onto the tiled floor. "Statement? What statement? I was asleep. What in the hell were *you* doing?"

Mike opened his mouth to answer, and she interrupted him. "*You* go talk to the police. Explain why you and your team weren't on duty. I'm going to try to convince that Harding fella to investigate this."

"That's my job."

She scoffed and turned her back on him, grabbing another snooker ball. "Right. You're apparently shit at your job. Tell the Detective Constable if he wants to talk to me, he can come by."

Mike clenched his fists, then shook out his hands. "Hey, I was running security for Andy years before you showed up. You want to fire me, fine. I'll go." He held up a forefinger. "But don't you for a second think I take this job lightly. He was my best man. I would die for him. You need to get all the way off my back. And you should be running to the police station to give your statement."

Kirra took a couple of deep breaths. She shook her head. "I'm not going to fire you. But I don't want you looking into Andy's death. You stay far away from that."

"You think I'll screw it up on purpose." It wasn't a question.

She shrugged. "I didn't say that. But I don't want to be in a position where I can think that." She took another couple of deep, steadying breaths. "I just lost my husband. Leave me be."

CHAPTER TWO

Nick reconsidered and re-reconsidered taking Kirra up on the case at least five times on his twenty-minute drive back to his apartment. Ten minutes, if he took the cross-city tunnel, but the tolls weren't worth the time savings. And his toll tag was bereft of funds.

He rolled to a stop at the kerb, took the local parking pass out of the glove box and tossed it on the dash. His across-the-hall neighbour was sitting on the apartment building front step.

Davie Sangster was what a casting director would choose as a stereotypical hacker. A little overweight, neck beard, brownish-orange hair in a short ponytail. He stood as Nick got out of his car. "Nick. Where ya been? Need a hand."

Nick laughed. "Third time this month. Either hide a key outside the apartment or learn how to pick it." He clapped him on the shoulder. "Come on."

He stepped into his apartment and flipped on the lights. He slipped off his suit jacket and carefully hung it in the closet by the front door.

He grabbed the small tool pouch that was on the top shelf and stepped across the hall.

"Timing it."

"Piss off, Davie." Nick crouched in front of the door and opened the tool pouch. He extracted a slim right-angled piece of metal and inserted it at the bottom of the keyhole and applied torsion. He followed with a long, thin, serrated needle-type blade and worked the pins. In less than twenty seconds the tension bar turned the tumbler and Nick stood. He turned the doorknob and pushed the door open.

"That's another beer you owe me, mate."

Davie smiled. "Deal. Thanks. That was a shade over eighteen seconds. You're getting slow."

Nick zipped the tool pouch shut. "Not a competition. Catch you later, okay?"

He returned to his apartment and slid the tool pouch onto the closet top shelf.

The apartment was in an ideal location if, and only if, the amount you paid on the lease was your primary concern. Coming into the apartment, the coat closet was to the immediate left. Just beyond it, on the same wall, was a small stand for shoes and boots. A few steps in, and to the right, was the entrance to the small kitchen. The cooktop and oven were exactly opposite the entrance to the kitchen, the sink and small dishwasher on the left and the refrigerator and a short counter on the right.

Beyond the sink was a half wall/counter overlooking the small living room, where an old sofa, two easy chairs, and a coffee table were all arranged to focus on the small flatscreen television mounted on the wall. Beyond the living room to the left was the bedroom.

He reached in the fridge, hesitated by the beer, then grabbed a half empty litre of orange juice. He sat on the sofa, kicked up his feet up on the coffee table, slid his laptop to the left a bit with his foot, and turned on the television.

Sky News was just finishing their lead story, the brutal beating of Andy Goh and discussions about the future of his electric car company, Dvorak Kars. Nick swallowed a mouthful of juice. "All those billions of dollars and he ends up beat to death and left in a pool of blood. And I thought I was the unlucky one."

He finished the juice and tossed the plastic bottle in the recycle bin. He turned on the electric kettle and stared into the cupboard above the cook top. "Prawn or chicken?" He sighed and pulled the top off of the tub of prawn flavoured instant noodles. He was stirring the boiled water in with a fork when someone knocked on his door.

He frowned and checked the time. "Hang on a second."

He stirred his noodles as he slowly walked to the door. "Davie? You lock yourself out again?"

A woman's voice called out. "You going to open up?"

Nick smiled and stuck the fork in the noodles and opened the door. "Kirra. You followed me? I'm flattered." He held the door open. "Not as nice as your place, but I call it home. For now. Can I interest you in a faux-oriental noodle dish?"

She gave him an autopilot smile and took the chair he had just vacated. "As good as that smells, nothing for me, thanks."

He grunted and shovelled another forkful of noodles in his mouth. "Are you sure?" he asked as he chewed. "I've got a chicken flavoured one left. I can get it for you if you want."

Kirra shook her head. "I'm fine. Really."

"If you didn't come for my fantastic cooking, then what brings you here?" Nick sat on the sofa at right angles to her. His living room wasn't even the size of her foyer, but she looked as comfortable in his domicile as he did in hers.

"I want to find out why my husband hired you." She held up her hand. "Sorry. Wanted to hire you."

Nick ate and shrugged. "I got an email. It was brief and to the point. Meet him for breakfast at your house to discuss a matter of grave importance to him." He held up his fork and clarified. "Grave *financial* importance."

"The missing money. That's not what I meant." Kirra looked around the apartment. The old sofa, scuffed coffee table, small television. "I know he wanted to find out why, and how, money was being siphoned out of the company. What I want to know why he thought you, specifically, could figure it out. Have you worked for him before? Had any other interactions with him?"

He shovelled the last bit of noodles from the cardboard tub into his mouth. "Never met him before. Read lots about him. Successful immigrant does good. Makes a motzza with an electric car than can get over 600 km per charge. Living the dream. Gorgeous house, " he pointed at Kirra, "gorgeous wife. Living. The. Dream. I was as surprised as you that he contacted me." He walked the cardboard tub to the garbage bin and dropped the fork into the sink. "Mystery within a mystery."

He sat back across from her. "How is it that you are showing no emotion about your husband being brutally murdered in front of your house?"

Kirra clenched her jaw and drew a deep breath in through her nose. "There'll be time enough for that later." She narrowed her eyes and cocked her head. "Right now I'm trying to figure you out. Andy is — was — a shrewd man. He wouldn't pick you to do this without a reason." She waved her hand around the room. "You don't seem like a successful investigator, if I'm honest."

"I'm in a bit of a slump. I'm sure I'll come out of it any day now."

She frowned. "Maybe Andy saw you as a pet project."

"I'd never met the man before. And my profile wasn't large enough to grab his attention." He grunted as he stood. "Wanna beer?"

"It's a little early, but what the hell."

Nick grabbed the last two from the fridge, twisted the top off one and handed it to Kirra. "Tell me about him." He opened his and sat across from her. "What do you mean by me being his pet project?"

She took a sip and considered Nick. Took another sip and shook her head. "He told me, on many, many occasions, that he could pick diamonds from piles of shit, if you'll excuse my language, with unerring accuracy." She cleared her throat. "And he has — had — a pretty good hit rate. Some of the executive in his — my — company were in dead end jobs at other companies, some of them non-technical, and they all soared at Dvorak." She picked at the label on the bottle. "I don't have any idea how he knows you, but maybe he thought the same thing. We'll never know."

"Nope. Never will." He chewed on the inside of his lip for a minute, considering how to broach the subject. "The hell with it. How did someone get past what I assume must be world class security to beat him to death at his front door? There's an aggressively serious gate out front, Mike the mini mongrel who looks like he could chew the leg off a horse, and cameras all over the place." He stood and paced. "I mean, there would have to be dozens of other places and times that should be easier."

She watched him pace and let the silence build for a minute. "I know. Don't you think I know?"

"Sorry. It's not logical. Does security live on campus, as it were, or do they run shifts?"

She was shaking her head before he was finished. "The place is a fortress."

Nick snorted.

She equivocated. "It's *supposed* to be a fortress. We get tucked in at midnight, the alarms set, the cameras spying and the gate locked. Murphy starts the day at 6:00 a.m. The crew he brings in depends on what's on the day's schedule."

"So, was this planned or was this a coincidence?"

Kirra placed her beer on the coffee table and stood. "The police will figure that out. I want you to find out where the money is going. That's what he wanted you for."

"I wouldn't know where to start." He smiled. "I'm more of a 'find evidence he's cheating' kinda PI. I certainly can't manage my own finances. How does he think I can figure our corporate financial crimes?"

Kirra smiled and stood, leaving her beer on the coffee table. "Come to the office tomorrow morning. 10:00. You can meet some of the team. I'll pay you well." She rested her hand on the door. "It's my company now, and I have a vested interest in making sure no more money disappears."

Nick closed the door behind her and dropped in the chair she had warmed. He picked up the beer bottle she left, half full, and continued picking at the label. "No point wasting this." He tipped back the bottle. "So she's the owner now."

He put the bottle back on the coffee table and grabbed his laptop. "Google, do your thing."

Kirra stepped out of the old apartment building into the warming Australian late spring and nodded at the man who drove her there. He was closer to sixty than forty, wiry and bald as a cue ball. No special chauffeur's hat, no special uniform, just a casual khakis and golf shirt combo, with ankle socks on feet stuffed into a new pair of low-cut Converse.

He held the back door open for her. "That was quick."

"I'm confused, Marty." She ducked into the back seat and pulled her seatbelt on.

Marty hopped around the front of the car and into the driver's seat.

"A permanent state for me, I'm afraid." He tapped the side of his head. "It's starting to go, I think."

Distracted, she shook her head. "That's not something I want to hear my lawyer say. What in the hell has happened to my life? It was sweet. A man I love who loves me for me, not my money." She sighed. "Now he's gone. It looks like maybe the company is haemorrhaging, and I don't know where to turn."

Marty looked at her in the rear-view mirror, a small smile on his face. "You'll figure it out. You have before. Every time." He pulled into traffic. He nodded toward the apartment building that was receding behind them. "You think he's going to get involved?"

"Hard to say. Andy wanted him. I told him to come by tomorrow at 10. We'll see if he shows."

CHAPTER THREE

Dvorak's lobby was on the 13th floor of a new, twenty-five-storey building in North Sydney. The lift doors opened and Nick stepped into a large open area with three of the more popular models of Dvorak electric vehicles on display. Up front was the two-seater convertible sports car in a bright fire-engine red, facing the lifts straight on, the stem of the letter 'Y' formed by the cars. The left arm of the 'Y' was a starter sedan and the right, a family station wagon. The nose of each of the cars faced outward.

The area was well-let, but not garish. A matrix of screens on the left wall played Dvorak television commercials on a loop, all of them emphasising the incredible lifestyle available to anyone smart enough to purchase one of these bleeding-edged wonders of technology.

At the far side of the cars was a reception counter staffed by a severely thin elderly woman with her hair in a bun, wearing a very modest dress.

Nick leaned into the cabin and coveted the sports car. With a vengeance. The seats and dashboard were covered with a light tan leather. The centre console curved up to the dashboard with a flexible touch screen. The screen was powered up with the local area map on the top half, and current speed, battery charge and other measurements he didn't recognise below. The seats looked to Nick like Recaro racing seats, or an incredibly accurate knock off. Close to $2,500 per seat, if real. "Nice."

He walked past the other two cars and leaned on the counter. He tilted his head and read the name on the ID card hanging off a Dvorak Kars lanyard. "Hi there, Doris. I'm - "

"Nick Harding, and you're waiting for Ms Roach," said Doris. "Have a seat and I'll let her know you're here." She cracked a very small smile. "You're three minutes early."

Nick waited for the rest of that sentence, either a compliment or admonition, but none came. He nodded and eased into a seat that looked like a spherical cup. As soon as he sat, he regretted it. "Dammit."

His feet were off the ground and his arse lower than his knees, which were currently knocked together. He grabbed the edges of the seat and pulled himself forward, grunting as he attempted to get his balance. "Jesus."

Kirra approached laughing. "Not very practical, are they? One of my husband's less than brilliant ideas." She watched him struggle to his feet, offering absolutely no assistance.

"You ready?" She handed him a 'escorted visitor' pass on a lanyard.

Nick adjusted his shirt and put the lanyard around his neck. "Thanks for the no help. How much is that sporty little thing by the lifts?"

Kirra cocked an eyebrow. "I've seen your flat. You can't afford it." She headed to the interior of the office. "This way."

Nick followed her to an interior staircase and walked up three floors. She waved her pass in front of the reader and pressed her thumb on the fingerprint reader. "Dual authentication. This is the finance floor." She held the door open. "Stick close to me. You're not permitted on this floor unescorted." She looked over her shoulder and smiled at him. "Security is staffed by angry young women and men who are frustrated at not being able punch more people. Don't give them an outlet."

"Message received."

She led him into a small meeting room. "Our conference room is tied up with a massive process mapping exercise we should have finished weeks ago. Needs to be completed before our annual audit in three weeks' time. Don't want you in there."

"I wouldn't understand much of anything, anyway."

"Don't sell yourself short." She sent a text on her phone. "Sam will set you up."

"What's he going to set me up with?" ask Nick.

"*She* is going to get you a company laptop with access to our accounts. Read only. You're not going to be able to transfer anything to your personal bank account, if that's what you're thinking." She had a small smile on her face.

Nick held up his hands. "Dammit. There go my retirement plans. What makes you think I can help?"

"I've done research on you. You, as the Americans say, are hiding your light under a bushel. Your background in financial crime with the federal police came with a number of high-profile cases. Fifteen years, right out of school. Then you left. I can't find out why, so I expect it's something unsavoury. But Andy trusts you to do the job, so I guess I can trust you, too."

Nick grunted. "Thanks. I think. Boredom."

"What about it?"

"I left because of boredom. Intense boredom."

"Sounds like an oxymoron to me."

The meeting room door opened and a head poked in. "Hi Kirra. Boss, I mean. That feels weird in my mouth. Sorry about Andy. Are you okay?" The door pushed open and a mid-30s woman with a buzzcut, overalls and a t-shirt, clomped in on Doc Martins. She slid a laptop across the table. It came to rest in front of Nick. A Post-It note stuck to the lid had the username and password.

Nick slowly stood. "Samantha Epping?"

"Nick. How are you doing? I was little surprised when Mr Goh asked me to set up a laptop for you."

"You two know each other, I take it," said Kirra.

"Undergrad classes together. You didn't keep in touch, Nicky."

He slowly sat. "Yeah. Drifted apart. It's been well over a decade. Good to see you again."

Sam cleared her throat and nodded. "Find me in the company directory and ping me if you have any questions. Our financial software packages are all industry standard. Based on your background, you shouldn't have any problems navigating them." She smiled. "I don't know what it is you're supposed to be doing, but boss lady here had me in at 6:00 this morning to confirm everything was set up. Must be important. Good luck."

"Thanks, Sam. I'm not sure it was necessary," said Nick. "I haven't agreed to anything yet."

She smiled and nodded at the laptop. "I'll bring the carry case with the charger and mouse around a bit later. First time you log in you're going to be prompted to change your password. At least eight characters, at least one number and one special character." She smiled. "If you use 'Passwerd!23' I'll personally punch you in the throat." She continued smiling and backed out of the door, letting it swing shut behind her.

Nick picked the Post-It note off the lid, read it and chuckled. "Temporary password is D0wnTownD!ck. She's funny." He opened the lid, and the laptop woke to a login window. He looked at it, folded the Post-It in half and slid it in his shirt pocket. He slowly closed the laptop.

"Sam's been here for almost a decade now. The network runs on her shoulders. Very smart and quirky. And funny." Kirra sat across from him. "I'm getting the sense you're not really on board."

He slid his hands over the lid of the closed laptop. Looked around the meeting room. It could hold ten people comfortably. A large monitor spanned on the wall opposite the door, with a three-camera webcam mounted on the top. A tablet on a stand in the middle of the table advertised a meeting coming up at 11:30.

He leaned back in the chair. "It's not like my calendar is full. And I definitely need the money. But, I don't know. I left the financial crimes world. It is mind-numbingly boring. And predictable. Someone sets up a fake supplier company, invoices for services not rendered or products not delivered, and has an underling process the paperwork so they can approve it. It's usually small amounts at first, then after a few months of not being detected they go for a big score. And that trips a ton of internal alarms, and they get caught. Or they attract suspicion by never taking a sick day or annual leave because they're afraid the fraud will be detected while they're gone. Or they buy really expensive cars and boats, well beyond their means." He pushed the laptop away. "Boring, predictable and barely worth my time."

Kirra shrugged. "Andy said money was being siphoned off by the litre and no alarms have triggered yet. And he thought you were the guy." She looked at her watch. "We're going to be kicked out in about five minutes. Strategy has a team meeting in here. I'll make you a deal. Grab the laptop and come with me to lunch. If I can't convince you over a meal, I'll find somebody else to do this."

Nick stood and tucked the laptop under his arm. "I could eat."

Mike Murphy unlocked the door on the side of the house and entered the security room. It was unmanned while staff was on the grounds. The night shift left at 6:00 a.m. A panel of six monitors was mounted on the wall above the lone desk. He entered his credentials in the terminal and checked the access log to the video surveillance system. Again. He had to have missed something. Logging for all south facing cameras had been shut off just before midnight the night before Andy's murder and had, miraculously, returned to perfect working order at 10:30 a.m., about 4 hours after the murder.

The logs were clear. The last entry before midnight was his, and the one before 10:30 was his.

And he knew with absolute certainty that he didn't turn off the cameras.

CHAPTER FOUR

"So, you don't take the lifts? At all?" Nick took what felt like the fiftieth left turn as they descended the internal stairs from the sixteenth floor to the fifth, where the company cafeteria lived. As they passed the eight floor, heading for the seventh, he started smelling the food.

"Gotta stay fit, especially with this food," said Kirra. "And it's all downstairs, Nick. Give me a break."

"My knees are shot. This is like a restaurant?"

"More like a cafe. No reservations needed. Some really good cooking talent in there, though."

They rounded from sixth to fifth and Nick was enveloped in savoury smells that triggered immediate Pavlovian responses in his salivary glands and his stomach. "Okay. This is something else."

Kirra pointed at a booth. She signalled to someone behind the counter and sat across from him. "Let's try this again."

"Just hold up a second. You have a hot food cafe? I was expecting a bunch of tables and a couple of microwaves. Maybe a couple of coffee machines. This," he shook his head. "This is better than most of the places on the street."

"Keep your employees happy and they produce quality results." She leaned back as a serving of eggplant lasagne was placed in front of her. Nick received veal parmesan and chips. "The financial health of the company is - "

Nick held up his hand. "Hang on. We're going to eat before we talk business. And I've got a couple of questions myself."

Kirra took a deep breath. "Of course."

He speared a chip with his fork and bit the end off. "I don't mean to seem indelicate, but if I was investigating this cold, just looking at the facts in front of me, you'd be my prime suspect. Rich husband dies, arty wife takes ownership of the company and is siphoning a big bankroll for herself."

Kirra narrowed her eyes. She opened her mouth to speak, hesitated, then smiled. "Valid points. All of them. Except for a few relevant facts. First, Andy and I were very much in love. And what a pair we were. An immigrant from Hong Kong and his taller wife of The Yugambeh people of the Gold Coast." She smiled. "Pissed off a lot of the older white conservative types. Especially when our net worth passed theirs. Second, my bank account might not be as large as Andy's, but it's large enough for me to live comfortably on my own for the rest of my life if I lived to 200."

Nick picked at his chips. "How'd that happen?"

"Huge, HUGE market for Australian Indigenous art in America. Huge. I do okay here in Australia. I could actually live a nice life in

Bronte on my Australian sales, but the American sales dwarf anything I can make here. I have a gallery in New York I visit every couple of months. No need to siphon off any money. That would take too much effort. And I wouldn't know how to do it, anyway."

He pushed the chips around on his plate. "Okay, that satisfies the money side of it, if what you say is true."

"It is."

"Okay."

"But I'm sure you'll check. Wouldn't expect anything different."

"Your husband was killed a little over 24 hours ago and you are here, in the office, showing no grief. No emotional impact from the death of the man you just told me you loved very much." He held up his hands. "Your words."

"None of us live forever. Life is fleeting. We're not here for eons, then we're born and we exist for under a hundred years, usually. Then we die and we're not here for more eons. We enjoy it while we can. You should enjoy it while you can. Find joy and peace in everything you do. I will miss Andy. And I'll grieve in my own way. But it was very likely that I would outlive him in any event. He was older than me by almost fifteen years. Plus, neither one of us were big on sentimentality. Live life a day at a time. Enjoy it while you can. Push through the rough days. You'll find, after a while, if you adopt that philosophy and adhere to it daily, you'll have a much less stressful life."

"Way too Zen for me. When's the service?"

"In a few days. He'll be cremated and I'll sprinkle the ashes in the ocean at his favourite surf spot." She slid a sheet of paper across the table. "A contract. $2,000 a day to investigate what Andy thinks is happening." She pushed the paper a few millimetres closer to Nick.

He didn't touch it. He didn't even look at it. "I left my cushy job with the feds investigating financial crimes because it bored the ever loving hell out of me. I hated it. Had a really bad performance review after completely not doing my job for almost six months. I deserved the sacking. It was the happiest day of my life." He cleared his throat and chewed on another chip. "And I don't think I can go back to it." He pulled the paper marginally closer with his index finger and glanced at it. "Let me think about it and I'll get back to you tomorrow."

"It's two grand a day, Nick. I know you can use it. And you can stay in my guest house while you work. It was my husband's last wish. For you to do this thing." Kirra pushed the paper a smidge closer to Nick. "Come on."

He finally looked closely at the sheet of paper. Picked it up and read it. A simple contract, binding him to Kirra personally at the day-rate she mentioned, until she was satisfied the job was finished, or two weeks. Whichever came first. A couple of paragraphs around confidentiality and reporting requirements. He shook his head and slid the paper back across the table to Kirra. "I'm only one person. I don't have a support staff. Nobody else works with me. I don't even, technically, have an office. I work out of my apartment. You need a bigger team, one with experience in this." He picked up his fork and knife. "But I'm going to finish this veal first"

"Nothing I can say or do to change your mind?"

He shook his head while he chewed. "I really, really could use the money, but I've got a rule about setting myself up for failure. Enough other people do that for me already. No point in volunteering for it." He took a bite and closed his eyes in appreciation. "And I try to avoid ripping off clients." He finished the last piece of veal and wiped the juices with the last chip.

She handed him a business card as he stood. "Call me with your decision tomorrow."

He unclipped his temporary identification from his belt and placed it on top of the laptop. "My condolences, Kirra. Hang on to this for me." He pointed to the lifts. "Do I need a pass to get to the ground floor?"

She shook her head. "Give my offer some thought."

CHAPTER FIVE

The regret started the second he sat in his car. Even before he started it and the small cloud of smoke popped out of the exhaust. The car started hard. He needed a new battery. The tires were getting very close to becoming slicks. And the crack on his windscreen got noticeably longer every speed bump and pothole he hit.

But he was nothing if not intensely stubborn. And proud. And unwilling to admit, ever, that he was wrong. He drove back to his apartment on autopilot.

But he was thinking now he was wrong. The financial tracking was easy, and the money good. But it was the contract that was appealing. "Two weeks. Twenty thousand dollars." He pulled to the kerb at the apartment building and turned off the ignition. The engine rattled for a few seconds before stopping with a bang. "Piece of shit." He tossed his parking pass on the dash.

The apartment was cold and dark. He flicked on the lights and turned on the small electric space heater. He filled his kettle and waited for it to come to a boil.

"Dammit." He re-checked the fridge. No milk. "Black it is." He spooned a healthy amount of instant coffee into a mug and was pouring the boiling water in it when someone knocked on his front door.

"Hey, Nick. You in there?"

"Shit," he muttered. "Yo. Davie. The door's open."

Dave lumbered in with a six-pack and took his spot on the end of the sofa. He twisted the top off a bottle and handed it to Nick. "Where were you this morning?"

He put his coffee down and took the beer. Wiped the condensation off with the tail of his shirt. "Turning down a job."

"You nuts? Ten bucks says the only thing in your fridge is a withered apple and sour milk."

"You owe me $10. No milk. The job was a non-starter. Lady wanted me to do some financial investigations that a good forensic accounting firm could do in a day."

"Why'd she want you?"

Nick shrugged. "Her husband wanted to hire me for some reason. She didn't understand why, but wanted to keep his wish."

"His wish? He dead or something?"

He nodded. Took a mouthful of beer. "Yesterday morning. Showed up to meet the guy and he'd already been pummelled to death," he said. "Anyway, they probably had a team of accountants in already going through the books. I wouldn't be able to do any better. Why waste time on something I'm probably never going to sort out?" He took another long drink. "Thanks for the beer. I owe you."

"Nah, I still owe you a few for getting me into my flat. You need the money, man. You should take it. Bullshit them for a couple days and make a couple hundred bucks."

"She was paying two thousand a day."

Davie choked on his beer. "Shit. Really? Dude, that's four times what I make as a corporate IT guy. Jesus. How do I get that gig?"

Nick leaned sideways and pulled Kirra's card from his back pocket. "Here. Give her a call."

"Nah. Not my thing. I got a job. Corporate ladder and all that." He chuckled. "You screwed up, man. Ten grand a week. You really need it, too."

"I do." Nick nodded and slid the card back in his pocket. "I really, really do."

"How'd the guy die? Wait. Are you talking about Andy Goh? Goh wanted to hire you?"

"Yeah."

"Jesus." Davie scratched his chin. "How did he die? News said very little about the circumstances."

"Apparently he stepped out of his house to pick a newspaper and one or more assailants kicked the ever loving shit out of him."

"A newspaper? *The* Andy Goh, tech billionaire gets an actual newspaper? A paper one?"

Nick shrugged. "Go figure. I was surprised too. Almost as surprised as I was that someone with the level of security he's supposed to have got hit that easy. Slipped in and out, cameras down, security staff not there. Seems like an inside job."

"You taking *that* case? Sounds more interesting."

Nick stood and stretched. He dropped his empty beer bottle in the recycle bin and pulled another from the case. "Not while the cops are looking into it." He twisted off the top off the bottle and spun it toward the kitchen. "You off today?"

"I got an email from HR. Way too much annual leave built up. Had to take a couple of weeks or lose it. I'm bored out of my tree." He reached for the remote. "You got Netflix, right?" He powered up the small television and pushed the Netflix button on the remote.

The television powered down and lights went out.

"What did you do, Davie?" Nick turned on the torch on his phone and headed toward the small closet in the hallway. "You pop a fuse?"

"I just -- I just turned on the TV, mate. Your fuse blew. Not mine."

Nick shook his head and open the small closet in the hall. He opened the small breaker box and shone the phone torch in. All the circuit breakers were still in the 'On' position. He slammed the closet shut. "Electrics bill. Kinda little bit overdue. Dammit. I knew I forgot something."

Davie stood. "I'll leave you the beer, mate, but if your television ain't working, no point hanging around. Come by after."

Nick watched him lumber out the door. "Well…" He fished the card out of his back pocket and dialled.

CHAPTER SIX

"You've changed your mind?" asked Kirra, over the phone. "I'm delighted to hear that."

"Not quite yet. I'm still confused. Have you had a forensic accounting team look into this yet? Because I think that would be the best alternative."

"Are you trying to talk yourself out of a job?" Kirra laughed. "No. An external audit team is arriving in about three weeks and we need this resolved before. Andy apparently believed you're the guy who can resolve it."

"Sure. And I'm low enough profile none of the financial media will get wind of it. That contract for two thousand a day, which seems especially generous, is that contingent on me delivering the source of the missing funds within a specific timeframe?"

"Come to the house for dinner. We can talk over the details tonight. I'll send a driver. The car will be outside your apartment building in an hour. No arguments."

She hung up. Nick pocketed his phone and sighed. "I don't seem to have any control over my life anymore."

An hour was long enough for him to shower, shave and get into some clean clothes. He sat on the apartment building stairs researching Andy Goh, Kirra and Dvorak Kars on his phone. The company did reasonably well until the Federal fleet contract. That deal launched them into the stratosphere.

The quiet tyre noise of an electric car caught his attention. One of the Dvorak sports cars sat at the kerb, Mike Murphy behind the wheel. The top was down and it was the sexiest car Nick had ever seen. Instead of the red that was in the office lobby, this one was jet black with red-accented black rims. The interior was lined with dark grey leather and the dash, where there wasn't electronics, was burled teak.

The seats were black Recaro, body-hugging beauties.

"Ah, Jesus," said Mike. "You? I wasn't told who to pick up, just the address. Sure there isn't anyone else here I should be waiting for?"

Nick stood, grin plastered on his face. "Nope. This is me. Company car, or does she pay you well enough to afford this thing?"

"Get in."

The engineering was exquisite. The door closed with a solid "chunk". The leather was kid soft.

"Quit gawking and put on your seatbelt."

"You don't strike me as the safety conscious type."

"I can't put it into gear until you put your belt on."

"Huh." He clipped in and was pressed back in the seat as Mike accelerated, silently. The car cornered like it was on rails. "Shit. Son of a bitch goes."

Mike's face showed no emotion. He ran an old yellow light and accelerated to beat the next one. "Hold on." He turned a hard right and entered the Cross-City Tunnel. "You're investigating Mr Goh's death?"

"The cops are doing that, aren't they?"

Mike grunted. "Supposibley."

Nick winced. "Right. *Supposedly.* Well, I'm not."

Mike glanced at him, then back to the road. "Then what?"

"I think that's between Kirra and me." Nick didn't know what Mike knew, or how much Kirra normally shared with him.

"Are you," Mike took a deep breath. "Are you reviewing the security arrangements at the estate?"

"What? No. Hell no. How messed up would it be for Kirra to send *you* to pick up me to review *your* domain?" He scratched the back of his head. "Okay. I'm doing what, apparently, Goh wanted me to do from the outset. He thinks money is pouring out of the company. I've got a background investigating financial crimes. I'm supposed to discover something your accountants couldn't figure out."

Mike noticeably relaxed. "Right. I heard him talking about that." They popped out of the tunnel into the sun. He squinted and lowered his visor. "We're there in five. I'm dropping you at the gate. I have to get into the police station to talk to the team investigating Andy's murder."

Nick glanced at him. "How in the hell did that happen?"

The security guy stared straight ahead. Took a couple of breaths before he answered. "I don't know. Too many things had to align just perfectly." He shook his head. "I really don't know." He took a deep breath and exhaled, puffing out his cheeks. "Surprised the missus kept me on, if I'm honest." He stopped at the open gate. Two guys much larger than Mike stood in the middle of the drive, blocking cars from entering. Mike pointed at them, then at Nick. "He's good. Let him in. He's meeting the boss. The new boss."

Nick hopped out. "Thanks. I'll see you around, probably." He nodded at the two big guys at the gate and jogged toward the front door. He slowed halfway there. It was too warm out and he was starting to perspire. Not a good look. He flapped his shirt as he approached the front door, trying to cool off.

The door opened as he took the steps up to the small porch. Kirra stood there, hair back in a ponytail and a drink in each hand. "Soda water and frozen fruit. Very refreshing." She handed him a glass and stepped to one side to let him in.

"Thanks." He took the glass, then swapped hands and wiped his hand on his trousers. The condensation on the glass was thick. "Where do I go?"

"Out back by the pool. Follow me."

A cool breeze caressed the palm fronds and ferns that edged the liver-shaped pool. A large deck area surrounded the pool. A covered area on the near side protected a rectangular glass table and six chairs. Hedges along the far side blocked the view from the harbour for those at deck level.

Nick sipped at his drink. Bubbles tickled his nose and an unexpected piece of frozen strawberry almost choked him.

"Wow." He coughed and cleared his throat. "Surprisingly refreshing. It's late afternoon, though. No beer?"

"Don't have any beer in the house. I could send out for some if you'd like. We're wine and gin people."

"No. No, that's fine. How are you holding up?"

A brief confused expression flashed across her face. Then the serenity mask re-appeared. "I'm doing okay."

Nick nodded and took another, more careful, sip. "Okay. But if my experience has told me anything it's that your husband's killer is more likely to be family than anyone else."

"But that's not why I'm hiring you, Mr Harding. I'm hiring you to find out where the money is going."

He nodded, slowly, and took another sip. He reached into his back pocket and extracted the single sheet, unfolded it and placed it on the table. "I haven't signed this yet, so technically you haven't hired me."

"Yet. You will. It's intriguing you, or you wouldn't be here."

Nick gestured at the expansive view. "Maybe I'm just here to look at what a shit-tonne of money can buy."

"You've seen it. You're still here."

He nodded in acknowledgement and tapped his pockets looking for a pen. She handed him a fine point sharpie. He held it above the signature line. "Just so we're clear, it's two thou a day, even if I find nothing." *Four times the most I've ever made in a day. Ever.*

She nodded. "And I know that's way more than you've ever made in a day, ever, but it's Andy's wish, and I need to respect that wish."

"Why the two-week deadline?"

She held up a finger. "The audit is in three weeks. And after the audit – and you must keep this confidential – I'm taking the company public. I'm leaving for a quick trip to New York in two weeks. You're finished before I leave, whether you find something or not."

Nick frowned. "I'm not going to hide anything for you. If there's fraud, I'll have an obligation to report it to the Australian Securities and Investment Commission."

"I want ASIC to know. I want it to be my company which uncovers this, not the auditors, and I want to be able to show our governance framework is strengthened to make sure it never happens again."

Nick sat back and crossed his arms, his brow furrowed in thought. After a minute he nodded. "Yeah. I can do that. I'll even throw in some recommendations if I find gaps in the governance."

"Write your bank details under the signature and I'll transfer the finds at the end of every day."

He signed and added his bank account details. Kirra took a picture of it with her phone, then opened her banking app. "You start today. There are still a few hours left. I want you to head to the office and catch up with Brent Slokow. He's our CFO. It's a starting point."

"Okay. I'll need a ride back to my apartment to get my car."

Kirra took a key fob from her pocket and placed it on the table. "I want you to stay here for the duration. I'm a bit of a micromanager and this makes it easier. Use this car."

"Lady, I don't know what in the hell you'll think I'll find, but this is incredibly, suspiciously generous."

She raised her eyebrows, a small smile on her face. "Suspiciously?"

"I'm a cynic. Wasn't born that way, but enough years doing what I did, and I can find an ulterior motive in everything."

"Sad way to live. I certainly didn't take any money from the company that wasn't legitimately due me. Like I said, don't need to."

Nick looked at her, saying nothing.

After a beat she cocked her head and narrowed her eyes. Her smile slipped a little. "You think I maybe arranged to have my husband killed? That's *really* cynical, Nick. The police have me at the top of their list of suspects. You focus on the money. We have big plans for later this year. I don't want to have to go to market for capital when I really shouldn't have to." She looked at her watch. "Brent will be there for another couple of hours. The address is in the car's navigation system. Security will let you in when you return."

She retrieved her pen and stood. "I know you're dubious, Nick. But I trust you can do this."

He watched her walk away. His phone chimed with a bank alert. Two thousand dollars had just been deposited in his account.

He opened his EnergyAustralia app and paid the electrics bill.

CHAPTER SEVEN

The navigation system had certain ideas about the route Nick should take to the Dvorak office. Nick had other ideas. The nominated path estimated a ten minute journey which was nowhere near long enough to sit behind the wheel of the Dvorak Carnival. It was identical to the model Mike picked him up in, but red, like in the office reception area. He marvelled at the car's responsiveness and took nearly thirty minutes to get to the corporate offices.

"I'm going to get too used to this." He parked in a visitor's spot and turned off the car. He brushed his fingertips lightly over the burled teak dash. "Waaaay too used to this."

The fob gave him access to the lifts to reception. Doris looked up as he approached. "Mr Harding. Kirra mentioned you'd be dropping by. I was expecting you about twenty minutes ago."

Nick smiled. "Traffic."

"It is a nice car, isn't it?"

He chuckled. "I'm here for Brent - "

"- Slokow. He's on the sixteenth floor. It's a secure floor."

"Yeah. Was there yesterday." Nick held up the key fob. "This will work?"

Doris maintained eye contact while shaking her head and handing him a black visitors card on a lanyard. "That fob gets our customers to reception. Wear the lanyard at all times while you're on the 16th floor." She placed a tablet on the counter. "Place your palm here and leave it until the flashing red light turns solid green. You need the card and one of your fingerprints to access the floor."

She waited until Nick's handprint had been recorded.

"Security will be notified if you're on that floor without that lanyard around your neck, and they haven't been fed in days." Her mouth smiled, but her eyes didn't. "Slokow is waiting for you in room 16.07. He's been waiting for almost thirty minutes. I don't expect he'll be happy."

"Fortunately, my job isn't to keep Slokow or anyone else happy." He put the lanyard around his neck and pointed at the stairwell behind reception. "I'll take the stairs. Do I return this to you at the end of the day, or what?"

"Keep it until you're finished here. It gets you in and out of the building after hours, also."

"But always have it around my neck. Right."

Three floors up to Sixteen. The floor was isolated from the stairwell by two security doors, one on each side. The doors, and the walls, were glass. He could see the layout, a standard cubicle farm surrounding the meeting rooms around the lift lobby. Private offices were at two opposite exterior corners.

His staring was getting some attention. He leaned down, pressed the security badge against the RFID sensor, placed his thumb on the reader and pushed the door open when it clicked. He smiled at the gawkers, turned slowly to get his bearings and made a beeline for meeting room 16.07.

It was a smaller room then he'd met Kirra in. A video monitor was at the opposite end of the table as the door. Two chairs were at either side of the table and one faced the monitor.

Brent was sitting on the right, laptop in front of him and mobile phone pressed to his head. "He's here." He hung up. "You're late." He was too large for his clothes. His suit was expensive, but tight. His top shirt button was undone and his tie loosened. He was at least a month overdue for a haircut, and his skin had that waxy look of someone who'd had bad seafood. He looked like the drummer for a bad country and western cover band.

"Can't be late if I didn't agree to a meeting time. You know why I'm here?" He settled into a chair across from Brent.

The CFO nodded. "Kirra mentioned something." He slid the open laptop across the table. "You should have kept this yesterday."

Nick took the laptop and turned it to face him. "Same laptop?"

"You should have kept it yesterday."

He closed the lid and placed his hand on it. "I've got some questions."

Brent looked at his watch. "It's month end and there's an external audit in three weeks. I'm a busy man."

Nick smiled and shook his head. "You've got a team. Knowing Goh, you've got a very good, well-paid, team. They're doing all the work and you're signing off."

Slokow leaned back in his chair. Sweat beaded along his hairline. "Maybe a couple of months ago. I'm very hands on, now. It's triple check the triple checks these days. Everything needs to be really tight."

"How much are we talking about?"

"I'm afraid I'm going to have to let you look on your own. I have a different opinion than both Andy Goh and his widow. The books balance. I will swear on a stack of bibles. A forensic accounting firm could take the books apart and find nothing out of the ordinary. But because they both think something is fishy, I need belt, suspenders and apparently duct tape." He placed his hands on the table and pushed himself to a standing position. "I think she's wasting her time. And yours. And, apparently, since I have to help you, mine. I understand you've got two weeks to find evidence of financial wrongdoing. Good luck. There's nothing to find. This'll be the easiest money you make." He pointed at the black badge hanging around Nick's neck. "Keep that on or there'll be problems. You've got this room for a couple of hours if you need it. Otherwise, just find a spare cubical."

Nick nodded and waited until Slokow left and the door closed before he pulled the sticky note from his shirt pocket and logged into the laptop. SAP was an enterprise-level piece of accounting software and cumbersome to the untrained user. It had been more than a few years since he'd last used it, and like all enterprise software it had gone through a number of upgrades since then.

He sighed and navigated to the Reports area. He had full access. "Interesting." He found the cash flow statements, the balance sheets and the income statements for the past three quarters. He drummed his fingers on the meeting table for a minute, then stuck his head out of the meeting room door. He tapped the arm of the first person walking past. "Hey, where are the printers around here?" He held up the black visitor's ID card. "I've got some things that need secure printing."

The guy pointed. "Over in the corner. Another one in the opposite corner. If your machine is on this floor it will only print to those two."

"Security settings? I don't want it printing out before I get there."

"It queues on the machine. Only prints when you tap your card on the reader attached to the printer."

Nick clapped him on the shoulder. "Outstanding. Thanks a tonne."

He ducked back into the meeting room and printed the summary documents for three months of financials. The software told him it took up 47 pages. "I hate this shit."

He closed the laptop and stuck it under his arm and wandered around the floor. Most monitors had polarised privacy screens on them, blocking the view of the monitor contents unless the viewer was within plus or minus ten degrees of dead centre.

Shelves of binders lined the partitions that broke the floor into discrete sections; accounts payable, receivable, payroll, inventory control, some others he didn't care to know. He gathered attention as he walked, but was left alone. He grabbed the ID card to keep it from slapping against his chest as he walked.

The printer, the one he found, was in a corner of the floor where the stationary lived. Beside it was a set of shelves filled with reams of paper, notebooks, pens, staplers, highlighters and every other thing an office flunky could want.

Nick tapped his card on the reader affixed to the side of the printer. The touchscreen changed to display his three waiting jobs. He selected them all to print.

He placed his laptop on one of the shelves and grabbed a couple notebooks and a fistful of pens. He stuck the pens in his inside suit pocket and placed the notebooks on top of the laptop and tucked all of that under his arm.

The printer spat paper out efficiently, aligning and stapling each report as they finished. Silence descended in the small corner room after the third staple job. He picked the reports off the printer and idly rifled through them.

"You're not going to find anything in there that will be of any help."

Nick looked up. "Huh?" Sam was standing in front of him, waiting for him to move out of the way. "Ah. You work on this floor?"

"Getting some expenses sorted out at the source." She held up her ID card. "Can I get past?"

He stepped to one side. "Sure. What did you mean?" He held up the printouts.

"We had our army of shiny-faced, eager-beaver financial people go over detailed reports with a fine-toothed comb and came up with nothing. I doubt you'll find anything they didn't just by looking at the summaries."

Nick tucked the reports between the notebooks. "You're probably right. Slokow said the same. But I've got to start somewhere."

Sam grabbed her two pages off the printer and followed him out. "Next steps?"

"I haven't finished the first steps." He looked at the time. "I'll take this back home and work on it there. I'll probably bump into you tomorrow, right?"

Sam cocked her head and looked at the laptop. "Where's the case?"

"Didn't get one. Or a charging cable."

Sam snorted. "Slokow is a waste of space. I told him to give it to you when he gave you the laptop. Follow me."

She led the way through the maze of desks to one of the corner offices. She knocked and entered without waiting for a response. "You have the laptop case I left with you, Slokow?"

The CFO pushed back from his desk and grabbed a case leaning against the wall. "Jesus, Sam. Wait for me to open the door next time, okay?" He tossed the case at Nick. "Everything's in there. Close the door on the way out. I'm still working."

Nick awkwardly caught it and shuffled the laptop, notebooks and financial reports into it and zipped it shut. He followed Sam out of the office and closed the door behind him.

"You seemed a little familiar with the CFO."

She snorted. "The guy's a moron." She grimaced. "That's not fair. I'm sure he's financially smart, but his social intelligence is on par with one of those squeegee guys at the street corner. They really can't read a room. Either can Slokow. Anyway. Great seeing you again. We'll have to catch up over coffee one day. I've got stuff to do. Later."

"See you tomorrow."

"Maybe. I'm IT. We're everywhere." She grinned and turned right, back into the corral of desks as Nick turned left through the security door to the lifts.

CHAPTER EIGHT

"Davie, you've got a couple of weeks off, right?" Nick tooled up the Pacific Highway, way out of his way back to the Goh residence. Or, he thought, the Roach residence. Goh had gone. His phone was blue-toothed to the car's audio system.

"Yeah. At least that, they said. I'm a corporate liability. Why? Want to head up to the Gold Coast?"

"No. I took the case. Financial crimes. I need some heavy duty computer work. Probably. It pays."

"Where are you, man? Sounds windy. And your car is still in its spot."

Nick took an exit, crossed over the highway and headed back toward the city. "I'm in a sweet convertible. Pack a couple of days clothes."

"Didn't say yes."

"Five hundred a day."

"When do you get here?"

"I'll be there in fifteen." Nick smiled as cool breeze washed over his bald scalp. "Maybe twenty."

The suspension on the small sports car was smart enough to accommodate the additional weight in the passenger side without knocking the car off kilter. Davie finger-combed his long red hair and smiled. "Sweet wheels. Swing past that chicken place. I'm starved."

"Food at the house." He glanced at Davie. "And there's no way in hell you're eating chicken in this car."

Davie looked at Nick, puzzled. Then his eyes grew. "The house? THE house? I've seen pictures." He chuckled. "That guy must have the most high-tech house in Sydney." He rubbed his hands on his thighs. "You've been there?"

"The guy's dead, mate. Show a little respect." Nick eased through the narrow roads in Vaucluse.

"I'm kinda stoked to be detecting with you. You got any leads?"

Nick chuckled. "I'm not going to find anything. A slew of internal accountants couldn't find anything. I doubt I'll do any better."

Davie frowned and looked at Nick. "So…"

"So I'm making $1500 a day and you're making $500 a day for the next thirteen days." He slowed to a stop at the gate. "If we find anything, it'll be a bonus."

Mike was outside the property, talking to one of the really big guys. He stopped when he saw the car. Walked to the front of it, between the number plate and the gate, and crossed his arms. "Who's the big ginger?"

Nick placed his hand on Davie's arm to shut him up. "This is my IT guy. Davie Sangster. Key to my investigation. I've cleared it with Kirra."

"Did you, now?"

Nick smiled. "I will. It'll be cool. Come on, mate. I need this guy to do my job. Paying him myself."

Mike narrowed his eyes, looked at Nick, then Davie. He took a breath, then stood to one side and nodded at one of the big guys. They entered a code and the gate rolled open.

"Thanks, Mike. I owe you a beer." He accelerated into the property and parked under a jacaranda tree. He turned off the car and looked at his passenger. "Let me do the talking with Kirra. She doesn't know you're joining the team."

"Team? We're two of us."

Nick grinned and knocked on the front door. "Yup."

Kirra opened the door with a smile that faded as soon as she saw Davie. "Who's this?"

"Kirra, this is David Sangster. Davie. He's an IT brainiac I need to help me." He smiled. "Out of my own pocket." He searched Kirra's eyes. "We good?"

She nodded slowly and smiled. "Yeah. We're good. Davie, is it?"

He nodded, looking nervous.

"I hope you're hungry, Davie. There's plenty of food."

Nick winked at him and followed Kirra in. "Plenty of food, Davie," he said with a smile.

There *was* plenty of food. They sat at a frosted glass table by the pool, enjoying the view of the harbour. Kirra started with pulled chicken tacos. "I don't eat beef. Not good for the digestive system."

"You've never had one of my wagyu steaks, done perfectly on a mesquite barbecue," said Davie. He chef kissed his fingertips. "Exquisite." He picked another taco from the serving platter and crunched a mouthful.

"Mesquite? It's a weed in Australia." Kirra sat back in her chair, picking at the salad with her fingers. She popped a half cherry tomato in her mouth. "America, sure. But here?"

Davie looked puzzled. "You're kidding, right? You can get mesquite chips almost anywhere. Toss them on a gas Jumbuck and there you go, right?"

She shrugged. "No beef. Chicken, fish, occasional lamb." She leaned forward and topped up her glass of wine. "Tell me, lads. What's your plan of attack? How are you going to find out *who* is siphoning funds, and *how*? And how much, for that matter."

Nick cleared his throat. "Well, it's a lot of accounting mumbo-jumbo."

"And IT wizardry, Nick. Don't forget the IT wizardry," said Davie, smiling.

Kirra looked at Nick and raised an eyebrow. "No bullshitting me, Nick. Forecasts had Dvorak cash flow positive this last quarter. Barely so, but positive. Yet we were almost $50 million in the red. I could see us missing by a little bit - the economy wasn't as strong as forecast, but that should have been more than offset by favourable exchange rates reducing our capital costs." She sighed. "I had a long chat with Brent.

He swears 'nothing untoward is happening'," she finger quoted, "but I want you to dig deep."

"You don't trust him?"

She held her hands up. "Brent has been with Andy since the beginning. I'm not saying I don't trust him. I think he might be a little over his head. He was fine while we were a small company, but we're big now." She shrugged. "Maybe he's over his head and can't admit it." She made a small gesture with her hand over her head and a young man with a tray of chicken satay and peanut sauce, slices of cucumbers on the side, appeared.

He placed it on the centre of the table. "More food, gentlemen? My name is Cameron. You can call me Cam. Let me know if you ever need anything."

The food was cleared and the three of them sat around the pool as the sun set. Nick and Davie each had frosty Corona beer with lime wedges jammed in their necks. Kirra nursed a chilled white wine.

"I have a number of guests rooms. Cameron will set you both up. He will give you the house wi-fi password and you'll have free rein of the kitchen." She took a deep breath. "I'm tired. It's been a very long day. Stay and work from here. If you need anything let me know. If I'm not here, let Cameron know and he'll either get it for you or find me and I'll get it."

Nick slowly placed his beer on the table. "Oh my god. We're prisoners."

Kirra laughed. "You can leave anytime you want, but do you have gigabit fibre in either of your apartments?"

Davie chuckled. "Nicky here doesn't even have electricity. I'm happy to stay here."

"Hey, I paid the bill. I've got electricity. Probably, by now."

Kirra clapped her hands. "I won't be here in the morning. I've got some early appointments. Cameron will get you whatever you need." She tipped back her glass of wine. "Good night, lads. I'll join you for dinner tomorrow and you can let me know how you're progressing."

Davie watched her walk out and cleared his throat. "Well." He finished his beer. "Wonder if Cameron has a new toothbrush."

Nick left his beer and grabbed his bag. "Where is he and what's the wi-fi password? I think I'm actually going to have to do some work."

"Nah, mate." He leaned back in his chair. "Sit. Finish your beer. Take advantage of this."

"I should get started."

"Come on." He pulled out a chair with his foot. "You don't get this kind of life very often, and this only lasts for a couple of weeks. Enjoy."

Nick nodded. "True." He took the offered chair and set the laptop case beside him on the patio. He opened a new bottle. "Cheers." They tapped bottle necks.

Davie looked around at their surroundings. "What do you think this place goes for? Three storey house, pool *and* access to the harbour. And what is this? 2400 square metres of real estate in the city?"

"More than I'll ever have." He walked to the edge of the pool. Underwater lights on the walls reflected off the surface. The pump gurgled softly. He kicked off his shoes and dipped a toe in. "Warm."

Davie jumped from his chair and gave Nick a push in the back. "Get in, mate," he laughed.

The bottle of beer arced into the pool, Nick close behind. He was taken by surprise and inhaled a mouthful of water when he hit and went under. The weight of his wet denims dragged him to the bottom. He struggled to get his feet under him, his lungs screaming. He fought to the surface and gasped, getting just as much pool water as air.

He was going under a second time when a hand grabbed the back of his shirt and pulled him to the edge.

"Jesus, mate. What the hell? Can't you swim?" Davie held him at the edge of the pool until he got his arms up on the deck. The depth - 3m - was painted on the tile.

Nick coughed mucus into the water and rubbed the snot from his nose. He took a couple of stabilising breaths and looked at his friend. "No, actually. I can't. Never learned." He coughed up a bit more water. "So, don't do that again, okay?"

"School swimming carnivals? Surfing? Weekends at the beach? This is Australia, mate. You can't swim?"

"Sue me." Nick lifted himself out of the pool and stood dripping on the deck. "Let's not bring this up again." He picked his shoes up and sloshed his way back to his room.

Davie jogged up beside him. Handed him his laptop bag. "Don't forget this."

CHAPTER NINE

Nick's bedroom was on the second floor of the expansive house. It was large, with a king sized bed, a desk in the corner with a couple of monitors, en suite and a balcony overlooking the pool.

Cameron handed him a slip of paper. "Wi-fi password. There's a direct port at the desk if you're sitting there. Faster than Wi-Fi. There's a robe in the closet. Get out of those wet cloths and leave them outside the door."

"Where you from, Cameron?"

"Up Galston way." The young man cocked his head and looked at Nick. "Why?"

"How'd you get this gig?"

"She mentored me during my first year at art college. We clicked. I help around the house and the money Miss Roach pays me helps out heaps."

"She pays well?"

Cameron shrugged with a half-smile. "Better than nothing. And look at this place. Better than any flat in Stanmore. Anything else you need?"

Nick cleared his throat. "I live in Stanmore."

"Oh, jeez. Sorry."

"Me too."

An embarrassed Cameron nodded. "Right. The cook has breakfast ready between 6 and 8 in the morning."

"I'm assuming it would be in the morning, Cameron. I'll see you then." He closed the door behind him.

He peeled off his wet clothes. He had to admit that the dip in the pool was refreshing, if not terrifying. The robe was a thick, soft terry. With a hood. He shrugged it on and dropped his wet clothes on a chair outside his room.

The laptop went on the desk, a USB-C cable connecting two monitors through an adaptor. He connected the power and jacked into the ethernet port.

"So. Gigabit speeds, eh?" He navigated to speedtest.net and checked.

Latency was 3 msec. Download speed was 983 Mbps. Upload speed was 853 Mbps.

"Huh. That'll do." He dug the notepad from the bag and followed the instructions to access the Dvorak accounting systems. Still standard SAP accounting software. Still the same boring rows and columns of numbers. He clicked through to the accounts payable files. Hundreds of suppliers, from silicon grommets to protect the wire harnesses transiting through the bulkhead to the batteries fixed to the frames of the cars. LEDs, screens, bearings, computer elements.

Fewer parts to account for, he expected, than an internal combustion car producer would need to manage. Nick shook his head. "Still, this is too much to start tonight."

He called Davie. "What room are you in?" He closed the lid on his laptop.

"A couple down from yours, I think."

"Where's the kitchen? I could use a couple more beer." Nick scratched the back of his head. "Can you find Cameron and grab some brews and come over? I'm in the one at the end of the hall. We'll sit on the balcony and spit ball some ideas."

"It's late, man."

"And we're working from home. I forgive you. Grab some beers."

There was silence for couple of beats, then, "Yeah. Sure. See you in a few."

Nick slid the door open to the balcony. The night air was warm. Lights tracked across the distant harbour, following the ferries and pleasure boats as they cut through the water. The Opera House was lit up with the colours of the women's national football team, celebrating the upcoming women's FIFA World Cup hosted by Australia and New Zealand. He stretched and sat. Kicked his feet up on the balcony railing and laced his fingers behind is head. "I could get used to this."

His room door opened and he heard the clanking of glass bottles. He looked over his shoulder. Davie followed Cameron, who was carrying a large bucket of ice with half a dozen beer jammed in. Nick smiled. "Most excellent, Cameron. Stay and join us?"

"Love to, guys, but I've got an Art History exam I need to study for.

Maybe another day."

Davie looked at Nick and raised his eyebrows. He pulled a beer from the ice, handed it to Nick, and took one for himself. "Another time, then." He dropped in the chair beside Nick. "Great view, mate." He tapped bottle necks with Nick. "What's up?"

"I started looking at the inventory, the suppliers, and there's too much there to start tonight. I want to take a step back. Frame up the problem. Most obvious suspect is the CFO. Brent something or other. Slokow. If, and I really mean if, there's money missing, he's the most likely suspect. Right? Has to be."

Davie nodded. "Occam's razor. How do you prove it?"

Nick looked around. "You think she's bugged the rooms?"

"What?"

"Bugs. Microphones. Cameras. What do you think?"

"Jesus, Nick. You been smoking weed again? You're getting all paranoid."

Nick placed the beer bottle on the table between them. "I don't know how to prove it because I haven't actually found any evidence. None. The evidence needs to come first. That's the problem. Hang on a second." He retrieved his laptop and sat back in the chair. "Do you think you can get into Andy's email?"

"I'd ask before I hacked. The Missus seems to want to help us. It would make sense that she'd give us access."

Nick nodded. "I'll ask her tomorrow." He opened his email. "Surprised he didn't send me any specifics. Just a mail setting up the meeting."

"You checked your spam, right?"

Nick clicked and navigated. "No, I didn't, actually. Fair call. Just a sec." He scrolled down a couple of screens and stopped on an email from Andy Goh. "Why did this end up in my spam folder when the other one from him didn't?"

"Does it promise four hour erections or to reverse hair loss?"

The activity at the warehouse started picking up once the sun went down. One person stood off to the side in the shadows with a tablet while pallet loads of batteries were transferred from a truck to the holding facility.

The warehouse was in a decrepit part of southwestern Sydney. All of the lights illuminating the outside were broken, save one, leaving a pale glow near the door. With Dvorak selling over 60,000 cars a month, the number of complete battery sets passing through the company pushed nearly 70,000. At a cost of nearly $2500 each per vehicular package.

Almost 175 million Australian dollars a month.

And they wanted a slice.

He looked up from the tablet. "Good work. We just unload the truck tonight. Finish the rest tomorrow. A few more hours and we break."

He watched the two workers move the pallets with the practice of a team who had been doing this for months, and getting paid well for it. He scrolled through his contacts and made a call. "Shipment is being unloaded. On schedule. No problems, boss."

"Excellent. Thanks. Let me know if anything untoward happens, otherwise I'll talk to you tomorrow."

Nick read through the email from Andy in his junk folder. "What do you think he means by this? *I'm of two minds whether I should get you involved in this or not. I've got a gut feeling there's about three to four million a month disappearing, and that kind of money invites drastic responses from those taking it, if interrupted. The breakfast is still on. I'll explain more in the morning and you give me your thoughts, but don't feel obligated to take this case. I'm putting together a summary of everything I know. I'll share it with you over coffee. You come with excellent references from my friends at the AFP. I value your input."*

He looked up from his screen. "Huh."

Davie tipped the last of his beer down his throat. "Sounds like he valued your input and wanted your opinion. You get a copy of that summary from Kirra?"

Nick shook his head and closed his laptop. "First thing I ask her tomorrow. Kicking you out," he yawned. "I need sleep. And to recover from the trauma of my friend trying to drown me.

CHAPTER TEN

A beam of sunlight inched across Nick's pillow, hitting his eyes at a little after 6:30. He groaned and rolled over, pulling the pillow over his head as he did. His mobile phone vibrated and wandered across the bedside table. He flailed for it, not looking, until it fell to the floor.

"Shit."

He swung his legs out of the bed and sat. Moved his phone around with his feet until it was in front of him and peered at the screen on the floor. A missed call from Davie. It took him a second to get his bearings. The bed was a king — the one in his apartment was a twin. The sheets were at least double the tread count he was accustomed to. And the view out the window wasn't the brick wall of the apartment building next to his.

He leaned down and snagged the phone and returned the call. "It's six in the bloody morning, Davie. What?"

"Pool. Breakfast. It's — it's beautiful." The call ended.

Nick found his way to the pool, freshly showered in yesterday's now clean and dry clothes. Davie had a piece of melon on the end of a dessert fork.

"Hey, Nick. Sleep well?"

Nick eased into a chair at the glass topped table. "What. In the hell. Are you doing up so early?"

Davie cleared his throat, then popped the melon piece in his mouth. "Well," he chewed, "we're on a job, right? No rest for the wicked and all that shit. We've got analysing to do."

Nick yawned and pulled a bowl of berries close. He spooned them into some yoghurt and gave it a stir. Poured a cup of black coffee from a carafe into a clear mug. He sniffed. "That is the best smelling coffee…" He smiled. "I could get used to this. But in about three hours."

Kirra strolled onto the pool deck in shorts, t-shirt and sandals. She placed her hands on the back of a chair opposite Nick. "Good morning, gentlemen. You're up earlier than I expected. What's your plan of attack?"

"Well," said Nick, "as soon as I'm finished this yoghurt I'm going to have a ham, cheese and rocket omelette and a second cup of this fantastic coffee." He ate another spoonful and smiled. "And then we'll get into the financial records and start collating any anomalies we find."

"You're good at this accounting stuff, right?" Kirra leaned forward. "Don't let me, or Andy, down. Got it?"

Nick nodded. "Absolutely. After I left the AFP I set up shop as a forensic accounting PI." He smiled wryly. "Kind of a niche market, to be honest. Migrated to divorce and missing cats." He frowned in thought for a second, holding up a finger. "Something else…" He snapped his fingers. "I got an email from your husband — it landed in my junk folder — where he said he was putting a summary together to go over with me. Can I get a copy of that?"

She shook her head. "Don't know anything about it."

"Ah, well. If you run across something along those lines, can you get me a copy?"

Kirra nodded. "Anything you need, let me know. I'll give you as free rein as possible."

Davie looked at Nick, then back at Kirra. "Both of us, right?"

"Yeah. I'll let the right people know." She looked at her watch. "I've got to go. Call me if you run into any roadblocks."

They watched her leave. Davie cocked his head. "How old is she?"

"No, no, no, mate," said Nick. "She's a client and recent widow."

Davie licked powdered sugar off his fingers and poured another cup of coffee. "So, what's first?"

Nick looked over his shoulder. They were clear. "Kirra."

Davie smiled. "She's not a bad looking woman."

"Again, tell me why she isn't my number one suspect? Spouse is always the number one suspect, right? Always."

"Dude. She's putting us up in this beautiful place. And the spouse being number one suspect, that's for murder. Aren't you staying away from that and just looking at the money?"

"Friends close, enemies closer."

Mike stood at Kirra's studio door watching her paint. He gave it a couple of seconds, then cleared his throat and rapped on the door jamb with his knuckles.

She continued daubing paint on her canvas. "What do you want, Mike?" She didn't turn.

"I'm popping over to the station to talk to the cops." He pulled a business card from his back pocket, glanced at it, oriented it so he could read it. "Detective Sergeant Richard Wallace." He grunted. "A real Dick. I'll be back this afternoon. Day crew is on point. Augmented with a couple of contractors. You'll be good."

She slowly placed her paint brush in a jar of cleaner. Sighed and turned. "You don't have to tell me. I trust your judgement. Don't make this thing a thing, okay? I don't blame you." She paused. "Let me know how it goes? Do you need Marty?"

He tapped the card with his thumb. "Not this time."

Mike knocked on the reception counter at the Local Area Command. A door on the back wall opened and produced a matronly woman in uniform who came in and sat in the receptionist's chair. "What can I do for you, love?"

He pulled out the card. "Can you let Detective Sergeant Richard Wallace know that Mike Murphy is here?" He stowed the card. "It's in relation to the Andy Goh murder."

"Yeah, I know hun. Dickie'll be right out. Have a seat." She sent a message to someone from her computer terminal, then looked back up at him. "How did that exactly happen? Inside his gates?" She shook her head. "Damned shame."

Mike shook his head and sat. And almost immediately stood as the door from the back opened.

Wallace looked twelve. Clean shaven, thick dark hair and an extremely charismatic smile. His suit looked like it cost upwards of $8,000 and his wingtips gleamed under the fluorescent lights. Mike stuck out his hand. "Detective Sergeant. I'm Mike Murphy. Head of security at - "

"Yeah, yeah. I know. Biggest case we've got right now." Wallace nodded toward the door to the internal offices. "Follow me."

He led him to an interrogation room and held the door open. The small room had a table in the middle and one chair on the side facing the obvious one-way mirror and two on the other side. Mike glanced up and saw video cameras in the two corners above the mirror. He shook his head again and sat in one of the two chairs with their backs to the mirror.

Wallace chuckled. "Love a sense of humour. Other side."

"Am I being interrogated?"

Wallace sat in the vacated chair. "We're just having a chat. No space in the office right now. I'm very interested in knowing what happened yesterday. You didn't tell me much on the scene." He shot his cuffs. "So, tell me. Start at the very beginning. Why weren't you inside the compound?"

Mike frowned. "Compound? It's not a bloody compound. It's a house with a gate. And a wall around it."

"And you need a security code to access the property, or be on a list the guy at the gate has, right?"

Mike nodded.

"Then it's a compound." He extracted a small notepad from the inside pocket of his suit jacket and placed it on the table. Then a pen. "From the beginning." He unscrewed the cap.

Mike cocked his head and appreciated the pen. He estimated it cost around $1,500. He took a deep breath. "Any chance I could get a cup of coffee? Black."

Wallace screwed the cap back on his pen. "Right. Give me a minute."

Mike leaned back in his chair and laced his fingers behind his head. He looked at one of the cameras and winked.

Wallace re-entered the room and placed a takeaway cup in front of Mike. He adjusted his tie minutely and sat again across from Mike. "From the beginning." He unscrewed the pen cap. Again.

Mike sipped the coffee and leaned forward, elbows on the table, fingers interlaced. "From the beginning. Right. Just before 6:00 in the morning one of the night crew woke me with a text," He opened his phone, went to the specific text message and slid it across the table, "telling me there was a fire just outside of the wall, a bit west of the gate."

"You sleep on compound?"

"I have a residence on the property, yes. It's not a compound."

Wallace glanced at the text and pushed the phone back. "So then?"

"So then I got up. Got dressed, quickly. I ran out to the front. The gate was open enough for a person to get through."

"But not a car."

Mike scowled. "Stop interrupting me, mate. I'm trying to tell you what happened." He waved at the cameras. "You're recording this. Get whatever you missed later."

Wallace held up his hands. "Go ahead. What next?"

"I get outside the gate. There's a Volkswagen Beetle, one of the old ones, burning. A couple of punks hanging onto their motorbike helmets are behind it, laughing. Me and one of the guys chased them while the others were trying to put out the car fire."

Wallace checked his notes. "Anyone call the fire department?"

Mike held up an index finger.

"Right, right. Continue."

"Yes, one of the team called the fire department, but the car was under the branches of a tree that grew on the property. We couldn't let that tree light up. There would be a lot of damage, and a risk it would spread to the house."

"Did you catch the, um, two punks?"

"You think maybe I would have mentioned that on the day? No, we didn't catch them. We lost them in Potts Point. They ducked through a shop and out the back door, I think. By the time we got back the fire was under control and the Fire Department had just arrived. As far as I was concerned, problem solved. It was almost 6:45 by then. I needed a shower. Technically I was forty-five minutes behind schedule. I walked through the gate and there was Andy, my boss, face down on the cobblestone drive in a drying pool of blood." He leaned back in his chair. "And then you came in."

"At any point did you think about telling the owners of the house about the fire?"

Mike shook his head. "I would have, if I thought there was any danger of it breaching the wall."

"What can you tell me about the two punks?" His $1,500 pen was poised above his notepad.

"Early 20s. One of them was tall, bald and had an iron cross tattoo on his neck."

Wallace stopped writing and looked up.

Mike nodded. "Yeah, really. He wore cargo shorts and a dirty white T-shirt. Converse high-tops. The other guy had a ponytail. Short one. Jeans and a black T-shirt with the Led Zeppelin prism on the front. They were fit. Ran like the wind." He sipped. "And they had helmets. Like I said."

"You hear them talk?"

"Yelling a bit, but nothing discernibly coherent."

"Australian? Foreign?"

"Australian."

"Did you see anyone enter the compound ahead of you?"

"It. Is. Not. A Compound."

"Nobody?"

Mike sighed. "Nobody."

Wallace scribbled a couple of notes in his book then flipped it shut. "Okay. Thanks. That's all for now. Let me know if anything else comes to you."

Mike pushed his chair back. "How do I get out of this place?"

"Tell your boss to come by and talk with me."

Detective Senior Constable Lizzy Lin stood behind the mirror, arms crossed, frown on her face. She watched Mike leave and Wallace pack up his pen and notepad.

"That fucking pen."

The door opened and Wallace entered. "You don't like my pen?"

"The thing was what, two grand? Ostentatious."

Wallace looked at her suit. "And how much was that?"

"Less than a hundred at Target." She nodded toward the glass. "What did you think?"

Wallace grimaced. "I don't know. I can't see a motive."

"Goh's security is legendary. Discrete, but formidable. Mr Murphy's reputation precedes him." Lizzy adjusted her shoulder holster, then her suit jacket. "I don't know."

"Me either. Uniforms are canvassing the neighbourhood for security video from the other houses. Should be hours of it in that neighbourhood."

"And the video from the compound?"

Wallace shook his head. "Our techs are looking at the system, but no, there's nothing. Need to find out who turned it off. Maybe they'll find out. Maybe they won't."

"We're going to have to get a bit more invested in this than that. The media attention is already beyond insane."

"Autopsy?"

She wrinkled her nose. "If we have to."

CHAPTER ELEVEN

Nick tapped on the door frame of the small IT room on the tenth floor. Sam had big canister headphones on and was engrossed in something on her screen. She didn't hear him.

He knocked again, louder. "Hey, Sam."

She started, pulled off the headphones as she swivelled her chair. "Hey, Nick. Your access card works, I see."

"Yeah, it's a maze trying to find people in here. What's this room?" He placed his laptop bag on an adjoining workstation

She looked around. A couple of workstations, frosted glass on the window. "Secure area where we run our cybersecurity checks. Usually two or three people in here. I'm upgrading software."

"I thought you IT folks pushed it to the machines."

Sam shrugged. "Sometimes ya gotta do hands on and local. Anything you need? Everything set up okay?"

Nick stepped into the room and closed the door. He sat on the corner of one of the workstations. "I need some help. I could probably get someone to set this up for me on the down low, but I need it clean because it's going to have to be in the final report."

Sam grinned. "Ooo. All mysterious like. Don't know if I can help if it's illegal."

"This is 100% in aid of what I'm doing for Kirra."

"First name basis. Huh."

Nick pushed on. "You know the CFO? Brent Slokow?"

"You know I know him."

Nick shook his head. "Not know who he is. Really know him. I've met him once. He's a bit of a dick."

Sam spread her fingers and waggled her hand. "Meh. We talk. He's starting to take Jiu-jitsu and wanted to talk to me about it. He talks a lot about martial arts movies. Big Steven Segal fan." She rolled her eyes. "Immediate disqualification."

"Does he seem like a straight shooter to you?"

Sam leaned back in her chair and put her boots up on the desk. Crossed her legs at the ankles and thought for a second. "He must be. He made it to CFO. You *know* there had to be background checks for that."

"I wouldn't bet on it."

"Why?" She held up her hands. "Not why wouldn't I bet on it. Why are you asking?"

Nick slid off the desk and sat in one of the office chairs. He leaned forward. "You know why Kirra has me here, right?"

"Obviously."

"Andy wanted me to review because I did a stint with the Federal

Police in the financial crimes taskforce." He shrugged. "Apparently the boss man did some research before he contacted me." He leaned back. "Hell of a thing."

"Did you get a chance to meet with him?"

"Yeah, nah. He was killed the morning we were supposed to meet for breakfast." He stood. "Anyway. The thing I wanted help with."

"Slokow?"

"Yeah. He's my prime suspect right now."

"Being the Chief Financial Officer."

"Right."

Sam looked puzzled. "What do you want me to do?"

Nick paused, thinking about how to frame the request. "I need to have a way to watch what he's doing on the internal systems at all times."

"Like a key logger?"

Nick grimaced and tilted his head. "More than thate. I need something that lets me see what he's doing in real time, a clone of his machine, and be able to go back and review what he's done when I'm not watching. I'll get Kirra's signature, if that's what you need."

Sam slowly shook her head. "No, that's cool. I'll get it set up and send you the link. Anything else?"

"Who runs the internal audit team?"

She sniffed and spun her chair back to the workstation. "Gimme a sec. I need to walk through the org chart. I can't remember her name." She looked over her shoulder. "She's in finance. Reports to Slokow. Not sure it will be an independent view."

"The report needs to be cleared by the Audit Committee and the Board."

Sam shook her head. "If Slokow cooks it right he could get it past them." She found what she was looking for. "The Internal Audit committee is headed by Jenna Mason. You want a trace on her, too?"

Nick thought for a second. "Yeah. Tell you what. Can you send me the minutes from the last four committee meetings and their working documents? If I need more I'll let you know."

"Am I your secretary?"

Nick fidgeted. "Well, no, but - "

"Messing with you, Nick. I'll send you the link to the SharePoint folders. You've got full access. If you can't find something, let me know. Okay?"

"Thanks." He stood and collected his bag. "Where does Jenna Mason sit?"

Jenna's office was festooned with skiing pictures. Dozens of them. Nick recognised a few from Thredbo, a couple from Banff and Whistler in Canada. He pointed to one of who he assumed was Jenna in full ski outfit and goggles standing on the slopes with Mount Fuji behind her. "Japan, right? Is that Niseko?"

Jenna was petite, with short dark hair and deeply tanned skin. She nodded. "Yes. That was a few years ago, though. I'd love to go back."

"Expensive place."

She nodded. "Who are you?"

Nick smiled and extended his hand. "Nick Harding. Kirra Roach has engaged me to investigate some potential financial impropriety."

She nodded. "What can I do for you?"

"You chair the audit committee. The quarterly audits show no sign of financial impropriety, yet Andy was convinced there was something going on."

"The quarterly audit test our governance systems. Makes sure everyone is playing by the rules, that compliance has picked up any new legislation, that sort of thing. It doesn't delve deeply into the contracts and financials. That's a much more thorough exercise. Some of the pre-work will start the week after next."

"What kind of pre-work?"

"Collecting all of the data in a pile. Inventory records, accounts receivable and payable, supply and delivery contracts, that sort of thing."

"Collection *should* take as long as it takes to push a button."

"Hard copy collection."

Nick nodded. "Will you be involved in that?"

"I'm not external, am I? There'll be a team of five or six coming in to do that full time, over a few weeks. Very intense."

Nick nodded and looked at the ski pictures. "Thanks." He pointed at the picture from Japan again. "Really expensive?"

"Still paying off my credit card for that trip and it was two years ago."

"Thanks for your help. If anyone is looking for me, I'll be in that closed off quiet area." He went to leave, then paused. "The coffee here any good?"

"Cups and machine in the kitchenette. It's got caffeine. It'll do, I guess."

Nick nodded, smiled and left looking for the machine.

The coffee wasn't bad and the quiet nook was quiet. And the link worked. He popped his ear buds on, listening to the early Beatles catalogue, and took a cursory look at the board's audit committee minutes for the past three quarterly meetings. There wasn't a single mention of Andy's suspicions. Not a whisper of a hint of something amiss. They weren't in-depth audits, though. The annual audit, to be presented at the Annual General Meeting would be much more thorough, as necessary.

He filed the minutes to a local folder on his laptop and opened the most recent batch of internal audit files. Again, and as expected given the minutes, nothing of note. The attestation signed off by Jenna Mason indicated that there was nothing out of the ordinary, that the controls were still in place and compliance was doing its job. Nick leaned back and scratched the back of his head, then jumped when an arm reached over his shoulder and pointed at the screen.

"You're not going to find anything there," said Kirra.

"Jesus. You scared the crap out of me." He looked at the screen. "Yeah, I kind of expected this. There would be no need for Andy to call me in if the problem showed up in these files. But I had to be thorough."

"What next?"

Nick looked around. They were alone in the enclosed quiet area.

"Already had Sam set up a trace on Slokow and Jenna Mason's machines."

Kirra nodded. "They'd both have to be involved. If either of them are."

"You don't think they are?"

Kirra sighed. "Slokow has been with Andy from the start. And he brought in Jenna. It's hard to believe they would be, and if they are, I'd be very disappointed."

"Give it a few days and I'll let you know what I find."

She rested her hand on his shoulder. "You have my full support. I want to get this behind me as quickly as possible."

CHAPTER TWELVE

Wallace pulled open the door for Lin. A waft of strongly disinfected air billowed out of the autopsy rooms.

"I hate that smell."

Wallace walked in behind her. "How many years you been doing this?"

"Doesn't matter. I'll never get used to it. Why don't we just read the report?"

"Because Cuttey won't get it to us until tomorrow, if we're lucky. More likely the day after. And I'll have questions. Better face to face."

Lin grimaced. "You unfortunately make sense." She pushed open the door at the end of the hall. A tall, gangly looking woman with her frizzy red hair in a pony-tail and frameless glasses on the end of her nose looked up from her desk.

"Dr Gail Cuttey. Have you met my partner?" Wallace reached out to shake Cuttey's hand.

She stood and smiled at Lin. "Haven't seen you around here before."

"Detective Constable Lin. Nice to meet you Doc. We're here - "

"Andy Goh. I know. Highest profile case I've had in years." She nodded at the table on the far end of the room. "I've prepped for you."

Wallace and Lin followed Cuttey to the table. Goh's head was balanced on a rubber support, elevating it. The standard autopsy Y-incision had been stitched up. Goh's body had been washed, and the bruising around his face and upper body was still very evident. The scalp had been peeled back from the top of his head and the top portion of the skull removed.

Wallace leaned close to Goh's head. "Removed his skull cap?"

"Of course." Cuttey picked up a folder. "Two blows to his head. The first one was a very hard blow from a right handed person at the base of his skull. Goh is — was — only 160 cm tall. Whoever did this wasn't much taller based on the angle of impact."

"And that killed him?" asked Wallace

"No. I said there were two blows to the head. The first one, near the base of the skull, didn't kill him but surely rendered him unconscious. The second one shattered his skull. Drove large shards into his brain. He bled into his cranial cavity. That one killed him almost instantly."

Lin pointed at his face and chest. "The bruises? He'd have to be alive for the bruises to show."

"Yeah. It was a rage-induced frenzy. Probably more than one. Kicked the tripe out of him as he died. Multiple broken ribs, broken right radius and ulna, bruised spleen, left kidney and liver, fractures to his nose, right orbital socket and both patellae shattered."

They stood in silence for a moment. "Knock him down with one whack to the head, kick the shit out of him, then finish him off with a second crack to the noggin?" asked Lin, scribbling in her notebook.

Cuttey nodded. "It'll all be in my report."

Wallace cleared his throat. "Tox screen?"

"Waiting for the results but I'd bet money it'll be clean. No processed food in his stomach contents. Lots of media about his healthy lifestyle, too."

He snorted. "PR is not truth."

Cuttey continued. "Skin tone was good and musculature advanced for someone his age. But I'll let you know when the toxicology report comes in."

"When will that be?"

"Lin, is it? Late today, early tomorrow. Lab is running with it now. High priority."

Wallace tilted his head and looked at the bruising on Goh's chest. "You said more than one. Could you tell anything from the bruising?"

"This isn't that TV show, CSI. Some speculative work here. It looks like maybe two people. Different sized boot. Lots of overlapping strikes. Ribs three through eight on both sides are at the very least fractured. Most are completely broken." She shook her head. "That would have killed him eventually if the blow to the head didn't. He would have bled out." She looked at Lin, writing furiously in her notepad. "You don't need to take notes. It'll all be in the report."

Lin looked up while she kept writing. "All good. What hit him on the head?"

"That's for you lot to figure out." Cuttey picked a plaster mould off her desk. "Looks like the edge of a cricket bat, or a crowbar. My bet is on the crowbar. There were no signs of wood in his hair. A hit that hard I'd have expected a couple of splinters at least."

"Crowbar, I'd expect metal fragments."

Cuttey shrugged. "Possibly. Not as likely." She held up the plaster cast. "But if you find a murder weapon it'll match this."

Lin flipped her notebook closed. "Great. Get that report to us soonest." She took the cast, wrinkled her nose and turned to Wallace. "Let's go."

CHAPTER THIRTEEN

Nick placed his computer bag on the table by Kirra's pool and sat back in the chair. Davie was head down in his laptop, barely acknowledging Nick's arrival while his fingers skated across the keyboard.

"What are you finding?" asked Nick.

Nothing. His friend kept clattering at the keyboard.

Nick snapped his fingers. "Yo, Davie. You find something?"

Davie held up an index finger for a second, then continued at the keyboard, ending with a flourish. He turned in his chair, looked at Nick and smiled.

"Well?"

Davie shook his head. "Nada. Diddly-squat. Clean as the proverbial whistle."

Nick sighed and rubbed his shiny scalp. "Why are you smiling, mate?"

"A whistle," smiled Davie. "Not a single bit out of place."

"Too clean?"

"Way too clean," nodded Davie. "If he's doing anything nefarious it's on a different machine."

"What about Jenna Mason?"

"I went through the quarterly audit work that she did. There's absolutely no indication that she was doing anything other than normal audit committee work. Have you talked to her?"

Nick nodded. "Seems like one of those workhorse types, saving money for expensive ski trips."

"We'll focus on Slokow for now."

"How deep did you dig?" Nick opened his bag and pulled out his laptop. "The key logger has only been in place for a couple of hours." He lifted the lid and logged on to the machine. "He can't have done much in two hours."

"Nah, mate. I didn't look at his key logging once he unlocked his laptop. I used his credentials and cracked his box. I've been wading through his emails, browser history, most of what is on his local and cloud drives."

"Too much to hope for him doing it that blatantly, I guess." Nick crossed his arms. "What were you actually looking for?"

"The usual. Emails with specific keywords, local copies of financial files which don't match official, encrypted messaging apps. You know." He scratched the scruff he called a beard. "We should be doing the same on the wife's machine."

"Kirra's?"

Davie grimaced. "Yeah." He looked around. "Can't say I'm entirely comfortable with that."

"Don't worry about it. It'll most likely be a waste of our time."

"You're getting paid by the day. Invoice a couple of days checking her out. Where's the harm?"

Nick raised his eyebrows and grunted. "She's paying the bill. I'd say there's tons of potential harm." He sighed and closed his lid. "But I guess she doesn't have to know. Can you get into her laptop remotely?"

"If she has a work laptop. I get the impression she hasn't been that dialled in. The exploit Sam set up on this finance guy's machine is pretty basic. And flawed. I can get into anyone's machine connected to the company network now."

Nick closed his eyes in thought.

"It's a big step, mate."

Nick nodded. "It is. Do it anyway. And see if Andy's machine is still connected somewhere. It could be used to bypass anything we're looking at." He took a deep breath and exhaled slowly through his nose. "What do you have that can monitor their personal machines?"

Davie rummaged through his laptop bag, extracting half a dozen thumb drives. He examined a couple before holding one up. "Plug this into any Windows laptop for ten seconds and I have complete remote control of it." He held another one up. "Same for Mac machines." He looked at it and grimaced. "Takes almost five minutes to set it up on the Mac, though. We going to ask?"

"That would defeat the purpose, Davie." He placed his hands on the table and pushed himself back. "We need to sort out the logistics of this."

His friend looked at the time on his laptop. "She's gone to the police station to give her statement. We've probably got a little time."

Kirra folded herself onto the metal chair in the interrogation room. Wallace waited until she was settled, then sat across from her.

"Do we need to do this in here?" she asked.

Wallace adjusted himself awkwardly. "We're jammed up this morning. Better in here than in the bullpen with some of the dregs the boys have dragged in." He held up his hands. "This isn't an interrogation. Really. We just want you to tell us everything you remember from the morning."

"We?"

Wallace looked at the empty chair beside him. "My partner is chasing a lead. If she gets back before we finish I'll introduce you." He flipped open his notepad. "Where were you when your husband was killed?"

Kirra narrowed her eyes. "A bit blunt, mate."

He shrugged. "Not here to make friends. I'm here to find out who killed your husband, make sure he is brought to justice, bringing peace to you and your family."

"Or she."

"Whazzat?"

"Make sure he or <u>she</u> is brought to justice."

"It was a pretty comprehensive beating. The autopsy showed severe blunt trauma to the back of the head and a host of peri-mortem injuries before the killing shot to the top of his head." He opened the case folder and read from the top sheet. "Multiple broken ribs, broken right radius and ulna, bruised spleen, left kidney and liver, fractures to his nose, right orbital socket and both patellae shattered."

He closed the folder and looked up at her. "A lot of fury from a strong person."

Kirra's eyes were closed and her head was in her hands. "Oh, my god."

He grimaced and flipped the folder over. "Sorry for that. Can we continue? Who was this angry with your husband?"

A tear rolled down her cheek. She lifted her head and stared daggers at him. Sniffed and rubbed the tear away with the heel of her hand. She slowly placed her hands on the table and clenched both fists.

"Anybody?" he prompted.

Her voice was strained through her clench jaw. "Nobody. Though that really describes how I feel about you right now."

"I'm really sorry, but I tend to be blunt and to the point. Occupational hazard. Nobody?"

She shook her head. "Not a single person I know who knew him felt this way about Andy. He wasn't loved by all. Nobody is. But the disagreements he had were never at the 'kill him' level."

Wallace nodded. "Where were you?"

"When?"

He rested his hand on the case folder and tapped it with his fingers.

"Ah. In bed. Had a late return from LA. Flight QF 41."

"What were you doing in Los Angeles?"

"Nothing." She gave a half smile at the look on Wallace's face. "I was in New York at a show in my gallery. The flight back routes through LA."

Wallace wrote in his pad. "Qantas QF 41?"

She nodded.

"You have proof of that?"

"I've got the boarding pass stub, and my accountant has the invoice for the ticket."

"What time did it land?"

"Scheduled for 12:30 am, but landed an hour late, just after 1:30 in the morning. I have an Uber receipt on my phone if you need that, too." She held up her phone. "I was dead. I can't sleep on airplanes."

The interrogation room door opened and Lin sat beside Wallace. "Where are we?"

"Finished. Ms Roach is of little value to our investigation." Wallace held a hand up toward Kirra and smiled. "That's a good thing."

He turned back to his partner. "No known enemies and she was asleep after a sleepless inbound flight from LA when the incident happened. I was just about to cut her loose."

Kirra stood. "Sounds like my cue."

Lin waved her had at Kirra. "Not quite. Please have a seat. I've got a question about finances." Lin smiled. "Okay, Ms Roach - "

"Kirra. Please."

"Kirra, as I'm sure you're aware, if you've watched any police procedurals, the spouse is the most likely suspect."

Kirra slowly sat. "I was asleep. He just told you that."

Lin flipped through the sheets of paper until she found what she was looking for. "You husband's net worth was recently valued at, conservatively, 3.4 billion dollars."

Kirra sighed and sat back, crossing her arms.

Lin glanced at her and returned to the documents. "The art press places your net worth at slightly over fifteen million." She raised her eyebrows. "Not shabby, but certainly not in your husband's neighbourhood. That's one hell of a motive."

She held out her finger, stern. "I. Was —"

"Yeah, we know. Asleep. Not the best alibi, if you ask me. Who did you hire? How much did you pay him?"

Kirra pushed her chair back and stood, hands flat on the table trembling with rage. She leaned close to Lin. "If you had something, you'd arrest me. Be careful what you say or I'll be suing the police department, and you. Personally."

Wallace watched the door close behind her. "Went a bit hard, didn't you?" He took the file back from Lin and closed it. "I don't think it's her."

"Of course you don't. She's tall, pretty - "

"Beautiful."

"Whatever. Clear your mind. Investigate this properly."

Wallace stood and tucked the file under his arm. "I've been doing this longer than you. I'm running her financials. I should get them this afternoon. But I still don't think she did it."

"The odds are in my favour. She's a spouse. He was far wealthier. Number one suspect."

"Twenty bucks?"

Lin laughed. "Make it fifty. You can afford it."

CHAPTER FOURTEEN

Nick leaned over Davie's shoulder as he hammered away at Kirra's laptop. They were in her office, the door ajar. Her artwork adorned the walls and a gallery catalogue lay open on her desk.

"You said five minutes. It's been almost 20," said Nick

"Patience, ass." Davie entered a command in the terminal window, closed the window and logged off. "I like the ascetics of Macs, but burrowing into a Windows machine is a hell of a lot easier. This will be like the finance guy's laptop - same access. We probably shouldn't access it here in case eyes see us." He slowly lowered the lid. "This was closed when we came in, right?"

Nick opened his mouth to answer when the heard a door slam and Kirra's voice bellowing. "The son of a bitches, thinking I killed my husband. Mike? Where in the hell are you?"

"Shit." Nick grabbed Davie and dragged him from the room, pulling the office door closed behind him. They sprinted down the hall and out to the table by the pool, sitting just before Kirra entered. Nick wrenched open his laptop and willed it to life. He looked over the lid at Kirra's approaching form.

"Are you two having any luck?"

Nick tapped on the non-responsive keys while the operating system came to life. "Plugging away. Setting the stage, really. Collecting data. I was about to say collecting info, but it's not information until it's been collected and analysed. So, collecting data." The password prompt appeared on his screen. He entered it and the login splash screen disappeared to reveal a terminal window. It covered most of his screen and mirrored what Slokow was doing on his machine.

He nodded. "Collecting data."

"Okay." She seemed to deflate a bit. "Have you seen Mr Murphy around?"

"Mike? No," said Davie. "We try not to cross his path. He's little, but scary."

"Yeah. That's why I keep him on." She looked at her watch. "What should I tell the cook you'd like for dinner?"

Nick looked over at Davie. His friend raised his eyebrows and glanced at Nick's laptop.

"I think Davie and I are going to head out and get a kabob and plan the next few days. This is all very beautiful, but it's a bit distracting. Is there a good place around here?"

Kirra absent-mindedly nodded. "Turn right out of the gate, cut through the alley about a hundred metres on the left. There's a decent independent place just across from the other end of the alley. Don't worry about the hour. I'll be in my studio all night, I think. I have some serious stresses to release. You've got the code for the front gate?"

"We do." Nick closed his just revived laptop and slid it into his case and slung the strap over his shoulder. "If we see Murphy we'll let him know you're looking for him."

"Don't bother. I was just going to vent at him."

The gate rolled shut behind them. "Damn, that was close, man," said Davie.

Nick chuckled. "Nothing gets the adrenal glands working overtime like almost getting caught while hacking your boss's MacBook. She said turn right out of the gate, right?"

Davie oriented himself with the map on his phone, turned right and pointed. "Kabob shop that way. Probably won't have Wi-Fi."

"I'll tether my phone. Lead the way. I'm starving."

"We eating there or taking it back?"

"There," said Nick. "We need a bit of privacy from Kirra."

It was a short walk, through an alley behind a number of other restaurants, skips and piles of cardboard boxes littering the way.

There were a few free tables. Nick grabbed one by the door and handed a fifty dollar bill to Davie. "Grab me a mixed kebab with chili sauce and a bottle of water, okay? I'm going to set up."

Davie snatched the bill. "I'm keeping the change."

Nick opened his laptop and tried tethering to his phone over Bluetooth. "Piece of shit." He rummaged through his laptop case and found a phone cable and connected it to the laptop. Still no connection. "Son of a bitch."

Davie fit the tray on the table. It held two kebabs wrapped in foil, two drinks and a pile of napkins. "What's wrong?"

"We're going back. I think the new OS update for my laptop has screwed up the tethering. It's not working. And I need to connect." He sniffed. "Damn. That smells good."

Davie shrugged. "No biggie. We'll be discrete around the pool. Better ambience, anyway. I'm getting used to her place. I'll get a bag."

Nick disconnected the cable and slid it and his laptop back into the computer case. Davie returned with a bag and collected the food and drinks.

"Short walk back. No big deal." He hoisted the bag. "But quickly. These aren't as good cold."

Nick grunted and grabbed his laptop case. "Let's go. Dammit."

They crossed the street from the kebab shop and entered the alley. They were halfway through when three people in motorcycle leathers and helmets intercepted them. Black helmet to the left, red in the middle and yellow to the right.

"Nick, what the hell is this?"

Red held out a gloved hand. "Your laptop."

"Piss off." Nick tucked the laptop case under his arm.

Black snapped his wrist and extended a metal baton. "Now." He was the tallest of the three, towering over Nick.

"I think they're serious, Nick."

"I think a retreat is in order." Nick turned and started running, Davie close behind. "Move it."

"Just give him your laptop, mate."

Nick redoubled his efforts to exit the laneway, thinking he was clear when his left foot was tapped into the path of his right and he tripped, landing on his face. And his laptop bag.

"Oh, shit. That hurt." He rolled to his back and instinctively lifted his foot and caught his assailant in the groin. "Ha." He crab -walked away and rolled and scrambled to his feet. "Shit. Keep up, Davie."

He had barely reached his top speed when he was grabbed by the shoulder and pulled to a stop.

He spun around and lashed out with a right jab at Yellow that didn't connect. He kept the laptop case tucked under his left arm.

"Just hand it over," said Yellow. "We don't want to hurt you."

"What? Are you nuts?" Nick looked past Yellow. Davie was prone on the ground, Red standing over him. The bag of kebabs was half under him, flattened.

Black took a glance at Red, then stood beside Yellow. "Laptop. Now." The voice was deep like he was trying to be Batman.

"Piss off, mate. Get a real job." Nick tried to see who was behind the visor, but it was tinted. "Take off your helmet so I can see what kind of bell-end is trying to rip me off."

Black sighed. "Look, Nicky, either give me the laptop now, or get the crap kicked out of you and I take the laptop. One way or another the laptop ends up with me. The only difference is whether you spend a couple of days in the hospital or not."

"Just give it to him," said Davie. He tried to push himself to his feet and Red heel-kicked him in the ribs.

"Oh, Jesus," he gasped. "Okay, I'll stay down. Nick, give it to him."

Black helmet stepped a little closer to Nick and held out a hand. "Give it to me."

Nick narrowed his eyes and slid the laptop out of its carry bag. "This?" He held it up, parallel to the ground. "You want this?" He took half step forward and jabbed the edge of the laptop between the bottom of Black's helmet and where the collar bones met the sternum, with every ounce of strength he had, trying to catch him in the throat.

Black had impressive reaction speed, though. He dipped his chin and the laptop cracked against the bottom of the helmet, jarring Nick's wrists.

Black staggered back, and grabbed the laptop, then swing it and hit Nick on the side of the head with it. The edge caught his scalp and split it. Blood poured down his face.

"Thanks," said Black. "It didn't have to be so painful for you, though."

Nick sank to the ground and watched the three helmets get on their bikes and ride away. He gingerly touched the side of his head. He pulled his hand away, spotted with blood. "You okay, Davie?"

Dave pushed himself to his feet with clenched jaw, furious, breathing through his nose. He pressed his hand against his side. "Couple of bruised ribs, I'd say."

Nick used the alley wall to help himself up. "What in the hell was that? They knew me and targeted me."

Davie shook his head. "What's on your laptop, other than what you're working on for this case?"

Nick shook his head and winced. "I need some Panadol. This isn't great." He touched the side of his head again and grunted when he saw the amount of blood on his hand. "Fucking mess."

"This raises questions," said Davie.

"He knew my name and where we'd be and that I'd have my personal laptop." Nick furrowed his brow. "Haven't been mugged in years." He patted his back pocket. "And they didn't even take my wallet or phone." He handed his phone to Davie. "Take some pictures of my head, would you?"

Davie opened the camera app and took some shots. "Why am I doing this?"

"I'm cleaning up when I get back to the house. I'll need to show the police what it looked like when I stop by there tomorrow."

"You should call them tonight."

"What' the point? They bell ends are gone. With those bikes they could be halfway to Campbelltown by now."

Davie handed the phone back. "Why bother with the cops at all?"

Nick scrolled through the photos. "Good shots. My head is shaped funny." He pocketed the phone. "I need to file a police report for insurance. At least I'll get a new machine out of this."

Davie picked the food bag off the ground. "Well this is garbage."

"Grab a couple of napkins out of there." He grabbed them himself and pressed them against the cut on his head. "You think I need stitches? The bleeding won't stop."

"Nah, mate. The scalp bleeds like a pig. A plaster will sort it out. Handy you shave your head."

Nick tossed the bloodied napkins into a nearby dumpster and held out his hand. "More."

Davie dug the rest out and threw the food in the bin. He handed all of the napkins to Nick. "Hope Kirra's cook is still on the clock. I'm starving."

"Look at my head again. I need to make a call about whether I go to A&E or not."

"Fine. Let me see." He turned on the torch on his phone.

Nick eased the folded napkin from his head and leaned forward. "Well?"

Davie peered at it, moving Nick's hand a bit to the left, out of the way. He angled his light on his friend's scalp. "I can't see bone. You'll be right." He moved Nick's hand back on the cut. "Just make sure too much doesn't leak out, hey?"

"Yeah." He sighed. "Let's head back."

"You lost everything?"

"I need to buy a new machine. Everything is backed up, though. I haven't lost anything. This was a miscalculation on their part."

They walked side by side through the alley and on to the main road.

"Any idea who 'they' are?"

Nick shook his head and grimaced. "No. Not specifically. Someone who is trying to stall our investigation."

"We must be getting close."

Nick barked out a laugh. "Not even. Hardly started. This makes not a lick of sense. I'm going to have one hell of a headache."

CHAPTER FIFTEEN

They stopped at the gate.

"You really do know the code?" asked Davie.

Nick grunted and punched it in. "Security isn't that shit hot here. Watched one of Mike's guys enter it. 8-5-3-2-1-1."

The gate shuddered then slowly rolled to the left. At the halfway point it revealed Mike Murphy, standing with his feet shoulder width and his arms crossed.

"Hey, Mikey," said Nick. He held up his free hand. "I'd shake, but there's this blood issue. Where's the best place for me to clean up?"

"Bloody oath, kid. What happened to your head?" His demeanour changed immediately from pissed off hard man to a solicitous father. "Let me have a look."

"It's nothing, Mike. Just need to clean up and slap a plaster on it. And eat. I'm starved."

"Yeah, the idiots who did that trashed our kebabs. We're starving," said Davie.

Mike looked at Davie's gut. "You'll live. Probably longer *not* eating kebabs, actually."

"Piss off, mate."

"There's a washing up station in the security office. And a First Aid kit. What happened?"

"Three guys on motorbikes jumped us and took Nick's laptop. We put up a fight but we were outnumbered."

"Was one of the a big guy with an Iron Cross tatt on his neck?"

There was a big guy with ink, but he kept his helmet on. I couldn't tell what it was."

Mike nodded and held open the door. "Come on in. There's a sink through that far door. Throw the mess you have on your head in the bin and come out when it's cleaned. Use the cloths in there. Don't worry about the blood. And it's going to sting."

"You think?"

Nick gingerly pulled the paper napkins from his head. The drying blood stuck them to his scalp. He turned on the faucet over the large utility basin and adjusted the temperature until it was almost too hot to bear. He ran the water over a washcloth until it was saturated, leaned his head over the basin and pressed the cloth to his head.

He repeatedly stamped his left foot. "Oh, damn that hurts." He pressed the cloth harder to his head. Held it there for full minute then slowly removed it. Rinsed it out and did it again And again. And again.

When the residual blood on the cloth was insignificant he dried his head by gently patting it with a dry cloth.

He left the bloody cloth in the sink and opened the door back to

Mike's work area. "You have plasters?"

Mike and Davie were sitting on either side of the room. Mike jumped up, popped open a lunchbox-sized First Aid kit and rummaged through the plasters. "Show me your skull."

Nick leaned over and handed his phone to Mike. "Take a pic, Mike."

"What for?" Mike took a couple of shots. "You're ugly, I can tell you that…"

"The police."

"Your friend told me what happened. Stole your laptop? Why do you think they did that?"

"Mate, I'm hungry and tired. If you're not going to put a plaster on this, I will." He grabbed his phone back. "Davie talks too much."

"I'm security." Mike pulled the wrapping off a plaster. "And you're officially under my care." He daubed some gelled antiseptic on the cut. "Don't move. This is sticky." He peeled the backing off the plaster and centred it over the cut on Nick's scalp. Stuck it down and made sure the adhesive adhered.

"Careful. That hurt."

Mike shook his head with a little smile on his face. He gathered the packaging from the plaster and tossed it in the bin and closed up the First Aid kit. "pp'You buy any lottery tickets?"

"What?"

"With what Davie said happened, you're lucky you only got a little gash on your head."

"Doesn't feel little." Nick touched the plaster and nodded. "Thanks for that. You think we got away light?"

"Yeah. You still have phones and wallets and the only injury appears to be a self-inflicted accident, not a provoked attack."

Nick frowned. Gently touched the plaster on his head and took a deep breath. "Maybe so. Thanks for the patch. You know if there's any food?"

"There's always food." He looked at Davies' gut. "Maybe not enough for him."

"Hey."

Mike had a small smile on his face. "I'll show you lads the kitchen. Keep it down. The Missus is down for the night. She's got an early morning tomorrow."

"I thought she was going to paint all night."

Mike shook his head. "I think the stress caught up with her. And the jet lag. She dropped like a rock."

The rider with the black helmet idled in the beach parking lot, waiting. Fished the laptop from his saddle bag. The case had a slight bend to it. It didn't close all the way. He opened it. The screen looked cracked, but it was readable. "Oh, well." He closed it.

A convertible pulled in beside the motorbike. "You got it?"

"It's bent." The laptop changed hands.

"What the hell did you do?"

"Needed to whack that Nick punk in the head with it to get it. IT was the closest thing on hand. You'll be able to get what you need?"

"You had to hit him on the head to get the thing you hit him on the head with?"

"You had to be there."

"I'm glad I wasn't." The car driver inspected the laptop. Opened it. The screen was damaged, but the lights came on and something disjointed came up on the display.

"You could hook an external monitor to it."

No response. Just a glare.

"My money?"

An envelope changed hands. A relatively thin envelope.

"Not much."

"It's what we agreed." The driver paused. "The team ready for tomorrow night?"

Black helmet flipped down the visor and started his bike. "Absolutely."

The roar of the departing motorcycle masked the noise of the laptop being upended into the trash can.

Nick layered ham and cheese on the rye bread. "This'll do, Davie." He spread mustard on the ham and ground pepper on the final result. He cut the sandwich in half and grabbed a beer from the fridge. "By the pool?"

"You're on meds, mate. Shouldn't be drinking." Davie finished creating his roast beef sandwich and grabbed Nick's beer.

"Yeah, no." Nick snagged the beer back. "I'm 'on' some ibuprofen. Get your own beer."

He wended his way through the house to the pool. Most of the illumination was from the lights under the water. Soft yellow lighting in the foliage added to the subdued lighting. The temperature was still in the mid-twenties at 11 pm.

Nick carefully pulled out a chair and quietly sat. "What a day."

Davie sat across from him. "You're at square one?"

"*We're* at square one. Except not. This isn't anything more than an expense. I'll pick up a new machine in the morning and charge it to this job."

Davie closed his eyes and leaned back in his chair. "I'm bloody shagged. You've been backing up like a good boy?"

"Always. To the cloud. I won't have lost anything important."

"The concern is with what they might find on the laptop?"

"If they can get through my encryption they're welcome to it. And they won't. Two factor to get into the machine." He held up his mobile. "Needs this, too. And they haven't been trying. I haven't received the authorisation code for the second step."

Davie looked puzzled. "Strange. Why in the hell did you put up a fight and get your pumpkin dented?""

"Well," said Nick. He tipped back his beer. "It really pisses me off when someone has the gall to think they can just take something that's mine." He burped. "I wish I was a fly on the wall watching them trying to get anything from it."

"Yeah, but mate, they aren't trying. You just said so."

Nick chewed the inside of his lip in thought. "Huh."

CHAPTER SIXTEEN

"Hey, Davie, I've got to head to the office to get my laptop set up." Nick leaned on the back of his friend's chair. "You need anything?"

"Nothing." He typed a couple of more characters then stopped and sat upright, twisting in the chair. "That's your personal machine."

"I need Sam to install the remote access software and a couple of certificates on my new laptop. It's many times faster than the piece of crap the company gave me. Seems almost like they didn't want me to find anything. Bonus points, I can claim it on my taxes."

Davie stared at the machine, deadpan, for a couple of seconds then returned to his own machine. "Boss makes the big bucks. Nothing in the world changes. I need nothing. I'll see you later."

"I should be back by 7:00 at the latest. I'll buy you dinner and we'll have a few or more drinks."

Davie sniffed. "Yup. That should buy me off. I'll be here."

Sam had can headphones on, deep into her laptop, bobbing slightly to the music pumping into her ears. Nick knocked on the edge of her cubicle. Then again. And again, harder.

Nothing.

He touched her on her shoulder and jumped back when she ripped her headphones off and spun on him.

"Jesus, Nicky. You scared the crap out of me."

"What were you listening to?"

"Music. What do you want?"

Nick slid his brand new laptop out of its case and gently placed it on her desk. "I have a new machine. Replacement for one that – was damaged."

Sam opened the lid and silently whistled as she looked at it. "Nice. Personal machine?"

"Yes, it is nice and yes, it's my personal machine."

She smiled and handed it back to Nick with a sarcastic smile. "Nice. Now let me get back to work, okay? I've got a lot to do."

Nick gently pushed it back at Sam. "This machine is at least five times more powerful than the Dvorak machine you gave me. Eight times the memory, and the screen is a couple of centimetres larger. I need you to set up the VPN license, the security certificates I need and the applications I need to complete the work I'm doing."

Sam let her breath out slowly. "We don't have a BYOD program here. I'm afraid that's a very non-standard request" She pushed the laptop back toward Nick. "Sorry, no can do."

He firmly pushed it back. "Call Kirra."

Sam held onto the laptop for a second, then placed it on her desk.

"Yeah, I'm not going to win that one." She opened the lid and stopped at the login screen. Slid a pad of post-it notes and a pencil toward Nick. "Password, please. And come back in half an hour. This is going to take some time."

Nick scribbled it on the pad and slid it back. "The last two letter Os are zeros." He checked the time. "Thanks. I appreciate you getting this done today. I'll be in the kitchen grabbing a coffee," he held up his phone, "and catching up on Twitter."

"I'm leaving in thirty minutes. If you're not here to pick up your machine I'm locking it in my bottom drawer and you'll have to wait until tomorrow."

"Yeah, yeah. Understood."

Sam waited until Mac left and squinted at the password on the Post-It note. Typed in the password and unlocked the laptop. "Virgin. Huh." She looked over her shoulder. She was once again on her own. "Okay then."

Nick poured a cup of coffee and took it to a seat near the window. They were on the tenth floor. The view overlooked a pedestrian mall. A busker had collected a crowd listening to his guitar stylings. Nick wished he could hear it. Some of the best musicians in Australia worked on the streets, independently producing music that should be getting drive-time exposure.

He set a timer in his phone for twenty minutes. He wasn't going home without the laptop.

Twitter was filled with the usual political tripe, TikTok dances and writers trying to flog their wares. He closed the app and sat back in the chair. Fifteen minutes to go.

Slokow slid in across from him. "Any luck?"

"With?"

He shook his head. "Finding out where the money is going. And how much."

Nick narrowed his eyes. "Still a work in progress, I'm afraid."

"You suspect me." It wasn't a question.

Nick grimaced. "I suspect everyone. Sorry, it's not personal. I should be finished in a few days."

Slokow took a deep breath and let it out slowly. "Debrief me when you find out what's going on, okay? It's not me. I don't expect you to believe me, but if you're even half as good at your job as you think you are you'll discover that shortly." He smiled. "I really hope you're at least half as good as you think you are."

Nick returned to the house with his newly updated laptop under his arm. It was just after 7:00 in the evening. He dropped it off in his bedroom and tracked down Davie at the pool. He was paddling on the deep end and hung off the wall when he saw his friend.

"Food and drinks, mate. My treat," said Nick. "Get dried off."

"I feel like a steak."

They ran into Mike in the kitchen.

"How's the head?"

Nick had his hand halfway to his head and stopped before he

touched it. "It'll be okay."

Mike grunted assent. "If you want anything other than a sandwich you'll have to cook it yourself."

Davie opened both doors of the double fridge. "When Kirra says she doesn't eat beef, does that mean nobody gets to eat beef?"

Mike pushed Davie out of the way. "Either of you know how to cook steak properly?" He took three sirloin tips out of the chiller. "Well?"

"It's a steak. Hard to ruin."

"She's hired you to solve some kind of financial mystery? And you're this dumb?" He turned on a cast iron grill and slapped the three steaks on a cutting board. "Watch and learn, kids."

"We're the same age, arsehole.

He glanced at Nick and shook his head. Mike ground rock salt and peppercorn on the steaks, flipped them over and repeated. Rubbed the salt and pepper into the meat. Dropped a couple of pats of butter on the grill and dropped the steaks on top.

"We're having asparagus with it."

"But I don't - "

"Shut up. We're having asparagus." He grabbed a fistful of asparagus spears from the fridge and tossed them on the grill, using a spoon to wash them with the melted butter and juice from the steaks. Tossed some crushed garlic and thyme in the mix.

"Medium rare, right?"

Davie opened his mouth to argue, then nodded. "Right."

He flipped the steaks over. "Someone get cold beer from the

fridge." He arrayed three plates on the counter and served up steak and asparagus spears for the three of them. He placed them at the chef's table in the kitchen and sat. "Well. What are you waiting for?"

Mike waited until they had their first mouthful of beer before asking, "How long are you guys going to be here?"

"Another week or so. You've known Kirra a long time?" Nick speared some asparagus and took a bite. "Not bad."

"Andy longer. Went to Uni with him. I had recently emigrated from Ireland. Tired of the pissy weather."

Davie looked at Nick and smiled. "Uni? What did you study to become a security guard?"

"I studied business, you fat fuck. I'd just gotten out of the SAS. I wanted to run a security business. A very successful one."

"Okay. Relax. The asparagus is better than I thought it would be."

Mike grunted. "Find out what's going on, okay? It really pisses me off that this happened. Someone get more beer."

CHAPTER SEVENTEEN

Nick cracked one eye open and winced against the bright morning sun. "Damn." He dragged the word out like it was being pulled slowly from his chest. He put his hand on his head and took a sharp breath. The memories slowly seeped past the pain.

He slowly swung his feet to the floor and looked around the bedroom. The pain in his head was a combination of hangover and the large lump on his head served up the night before.

He stumbled into the shower and stood under the pounding hot spray until he began to feel a little more alive. "I need coffee."

"You and me both, mate."

He whipped his head around to see who spoke and immediately regretted it. "Jesus, Davie. What are you doing in here?" He pressed the palm of his hand against his forehead,

"I can't see your bits through the steam. Relax."

"I need some Grade A painkillers. Think you can scare some up while I shave?"

"Sure, mate."

"And that coffee. Please."

Davie chuckled as he left the room.

Nick turned off the shower and dried himself, taking care around his head. He rubbed his hand over the stubble on his scalp. He really should shave it, but the thought of navigating a razor around the injury on his scalp was too much.

He wrapped a towel around his waist and checked what clean clothes he still had. Limited choice. He pulled on a pair of cargo shorts and a Chewbacca t-shirt and made his way to the pool. The sun was unbearably bright. He squinted as he moved the chair out of the sun and sat.

He leaned back and closed his eyes and had drifted to a state of half sleep when the smell of coffee — really good coffee — wafted past his olfactory receptors.

"Unngh." He sat up and opened his eyes. A large mug of black coffee sat beside a small saucer holding two pills and a bottle of water covered with condensation. He looked around, squinting, until he found Davie. "What are these?"

"Heavy duty ibuprofen, no codeine." He scraped out his chair and smiled at Nick's wincing. "Sorry."

Nick grunted and popped the pills. Tipped back half the bottle of water.. "I'm more pissed off this morning than I was last night. First thing's first — I need a new head."

"And second thing?"

"Tell me that the key logger you have is completely unobtrusive."

"The key logger I have is completely unobtrusive." He smiled. "Shouldn't you have asked me that before we put it on Kirra's machine?

Nick nodded. "Slokow is more tech savvy." He took a sip of coffee and smiled. "It's good." He took a deeper draught. "Okay. We need to get into Slokow's personal laptop."

Davie stared at Nick for a full minute. "Nick, mate, you're proposing we step across the line here. Company machines legit fall under your investigation. His personal machine doesn't."

"If he's doing something sneaky, it's not on the work machine. Ergo, we need to get into the personal one. Or 'ones', if he has more than one."

"That's breaking and entering. Serious time. And you'd lose your licence."

Nick contemplated that thought over another mouthful of coffee. "Then we don't get caught. I'm bringing you into the office with me this morning."

"Jesus," he groaned. "I'm going to have to shave, aren't I?"

"Did I tell you he found me at the office yesterday and insisted he was not the person we're looking for?"

"Suss. First on the list. But I'm already into his machine. You think he keeps his personal laptop at work? That doesn't make sense."

"We need to find out where he lives."

"Right. Bills or something in his office."

Nick knocked on the doorframe of Sam's office. "Hey, can I bug you a minute?"

She visibly sighed and closed the screen she was working on and turned her chair. "Sure. Who's this?"

Nick looked at a recently shaved Davie then back at Sam. "Dave Sangster, this is Sam. She's the IT guru around here. Davie's helping me out."

"Where's his visitor's pass? It needs to be displayed at all times and he needs to have an escort."

"We didn't stop by the front desk. We're just in here for a couple of minutes. I'm escorting him."

"Jesus." She stood and pushed her chair back. Grabbed Davie by the arm. "A visitor can't escort another visitor. You need to leave until you've got the appropriate pass.".

He pulled his arm free. "Relax. We'll go get one now."

"I'll be here whenever you get back."

Davie followed Nick to the lift lobby. "She's a bit off."

"Yeah, that was my bad. I should have known better." The doors opened on reception's floor. The three cars were still there.

"These are nice," said Davie. "Very, very nice."

"No time. We've got things to do." Nick leaned on the front desk. "Remember me?"

"Kirra's pet. What can I do for you? Your pass not working?"

"No, it's fine." He pulled Davie closer. "David Sangster. He works for me and needs the same access Kirra gave me."

"Well, I can arrange floor access, but IT access will need to be handled by—"

"—by Sam. I know. We were just there. I let Davie tailgate me in and she almost ripped my head off."

The receptionist laughed. "I don't see any bruises. You got off easy." She held out her hand. "Your driver's licence, Mr Sangster?"

He handed it over, then turned his back on the counter and admired the cars. "I could enjoy driving again, with one of these."

"You can't afford it, mate." Nick collected the credentials from the receptionist and thanked her. He tapped Davie on the arm. "Keep these around your neck or you'll end up getting head butted by Sam."

"Thanks." He grabbed them and put them on. He turned and smiled at the receptionist. "My licence?"

She handed it back, and placed the palm reader on the counter. "Place your hand here until the flashing red light turns green."

He looked at Nick who nodded. "Okay."

The light turned green and the receptionist retrieved the tablet. "Good to go."

"Thanks." He fell in beside Nick. "What now?"

"Down three flights to level 10 and start over. Be nice to Sam, okay? She's an old friend and can help us a lot." He started down the stairs. "But don't tell her what we're up to. I'm pretty sure we're going to cross the line of legality."

"Way across the line." Davie looked at the two separate cards on the lanyard. "Why two?"

"The white one with the big red 'V' on it gets you in every floor except Level 16, the secure floor. The black one gets you on to 16."

They walked down two flights before Davie talked again. "How we going to do this?"

"Get Sam used to seeing you around. You become a fixture. Need to accelerate that, so we'll bug her about printer location, stationary, a bunch of shit she doesn't really handle."

"Annoying? I can be annoying."

"I know. Crank it up. Then I'll get Slokow out of his office and maybe his personal laptop is in there and you spike it. If it's not, we'll need to get his home address and do it there."

"I *really* hope it's in his office. I'm not cool about breaking into his house. That's a felony."

Nick smiled. "You're too uptight. One problem at a time."

They reached Level 10 and Nick got Davie to use his pass to get in the door. "Making sure it works."

It did.

Sam met them at the door and inspected the credentials. "Okay. Why are you here?"

"We just popped by here to reassure you that Davie was set up properly. We'll be heading up to 16 to gather financials. Would you know if Slokow is in today?"

"He was earlier."

"We'll catch you later then."

They'd wandered around the 16th floor for almost an hour before Nick slowed by the copy machine. "Slokow's office is in that corner. I'll draw him out on some pretext and you check the place out. You're going to need a story if someone catches you."

"I'll think of something."

"Okay. Hang here until you see me pass. You'll have about five minutes."

Nick knocked on Slokow's door frame. "Hey, can I grab you for minute? I need some background."

Brent Slokow waved him in. "Grab a seat."

Nick grimaced. He glanced back at the copy room. "I was about to get a coffee. I'll buy you one. It's a bit stuffy in here, don't you think?"

Slokow looked at his laptop and then at his empty coffee cup and sighed. "Sure." He locked his laptop and pushed himself away from his desk. "What specifically do you want to talk about?"

Davie waited a couple of seconds after Nick and Slokow left. He grabbed the doorknob to the office and twisted.

Or tried to. The door was locked.

"Son of a bitch." He rattled the knob, an exercise in futility. "Dammit. Nick has got to teach me how to pick these things."

A young woman approached him, casually checking out the ID cards on his lanyards. "Can I help you?"

He finger-combed his hair. "I'm from, um, Dell. Mr Slokow had a repetitive BSOD error on his laptop and called our service centre. Actually your IT department called us after he called them and they couldn't handle it. I need to update a driver so his SAP software can connect to the distributed printer server." He looked at his watch. "We were scheduled for 10:30, which is now, but his door is locked. I've got a jam-packed schedule today. It only takes five minutes to load the driver," he pulled a thumb drive from his pocket, "but if I can't get in there in the next couple of minutes I'm going to have to bail to the next job. In Parramatta."

"So, he can't print?"

"Not from SAP. And his machine has slowed to a crawl. Look, you don't have the key, do you?" A set of keys hung off her lanyard.

"I do. But I don't know."

"You're his EA?"

She nodded.

"Could you let him know that I was here? My next available spot is late next week."

She set her jaw. Furrowed her brow. An executive decision had to be made. She extended the keys and picked out the appropriate one and unlocked the door.

"I really appreciate this. I'll let him know you helped."

Her phone chimed with a message. "Absolutely." She pointed at her phone. "I've got to answer this. Let me know when you're finished and I'll lock it back up. I'm in the next cube over."

Davie waited until she left then looked around the office. Opened a laptop bag leaning against the leg of Slokow's desk to check for a personal machine.

Nothing.

He flipped through the correspondence on his desk until he found a personal letter addressed to Sally Slokow. "The wife." He took a picture of the address on the envelope and left the office.

He tapped on the EA's desk. "Finished. Thanks for your help."

"Thanks for letting me know." She reflexively held on to the keys hanging around her neck and made a path to her boss's office.

He thumbed a text to Nick. '*Success. Need to go to his house now. I have his address. I'm by the copier.*'

CHAPTER EIGHTEEN

"Block the view a bit, mate." Nick crouched with his pick set as Davie shuffled a bit to the left. They stood on the front step of an old, double-brick two storey house in Canada Bay. Shrubbery on either side of the steps blocked most of the view of the front door and Davie's substantial bulk provided the rest of the cover.

Nick glanced over his shoulder, then returned his focus to the deadbolt. After a couple of minutes, it slid open. "We're in."

Davie followed him into the house, pulling the door shut behind him. "Nuts-o doing this in broad daylight, mate."

"Can't really do it at night. Where would his laptop be?"

"Where would his home office be?" Davie walked into the kitchen and opened the fridge. Grabbed a beer. "Probably downstairs here, right?" He twisted off the cap and tossed it in the garbage. "I'll take the back area of the house. You take the front."

Nick threw him a mock salute and moved into the lounge area. There were a large flatscreen TV, Apple TV box, Blu-ray player and a stack of remotes. Nice black leather furniture. Glass and chrome coffee table and side tables.

No sign of a laptop or desktop computer.

He checked in with Davie. "Any luck?"

"Nothing in the kitchen or laundry room, unsurprisingly. Upstairs?"

Nick checked his watch. "Yeah, we've got tonnes of time." He led the way up the stairs. Bathroom at the top of the stairs, two bedrooms off to the right and one to the left. Nick pointed to the left. "That's probably the office."

The front door opened. "Brent? Are you here? The door was unlocked." It was a woman's voice. "Brent? Honey?"

Nick pushed Davie into the office and quietly closed the door. "Shit," he whispered. "Forgot about the wife."

"Found both of their laptops. Both of them are Macs. This'll take about ten minutes."

"Get started. I'll keep an ear."

Davie opened the first laptop, stuck the thumb drive in the USB port and performed a hard start on the machine. "Shit. The start-up sound." He took off his shirt and bundled it over the MacBook speakers. The start-up chime was muffled, but still audible. "You think she heard that?"

"Keep going," whispered Nick.

Sally Slokow walked slowly through her lounge room. Nothing was taken. Nothing *seemed* out of place. But something felt different. She slid her phone out of her back pocket and called her husband. "Hey, did you come by this morning?"

"What? I'm heading to meeting. Don't have a lot of time to talk."

"You left before me this morning. I left last. Could swear on a stack of bibles I locked up. But I forgot to set the alarm. Just came by to set it and the front door was unlocked."

"Anything missing?"

"No. That's not the point."

"Then what is? Seriously, I've got to run. You must have forgotten when you left. Like you forgot the alarm." He sighed. "If nothing is missing we'll talk about it tonight, okay?"

Nick was out of the home office and up against the wall near the stairs, listening.

"Nothing is missing from the lounge room, but I haven't looked upstairs yet," she said. She sounded closer. Like the bottom of the stairs.

Nick treaded carefully along the edge of the hallway back into the home office. He gently closed the door. "Time?"

"Almost done with the second one," whispered Davie. "What's happening?"

"Missus is a bit suss about whether someone is in here."

"Astute lady."

"Yeah. We're about to be busted." Nick moved the curtain aside and peered out the window. It looked over the front of the house. And the porch roof over the front door. He opened the latch on the top of the sash window. "Hope this is quiet." He pushed the window open.

Quietly. A light breeze ruffled the curtain. "Ready?"

Sally's voice was getting closer. "Honey, I'm going upstairs." A tread creaked as she took the first step up, then she paused.. "You're nuts. There's nobody here now." She continued ascending the stairs. "I'd be able to feel them. There's nobody here." She reached the top.

Davie ejected the thumb drive. "Go."

Nick stepped out onto the porch roof and moved out of the way as Davie struggled through.

He reached past his friend to pull the curtain closed and lowered the window. The door opened just as the window closed. "Get down."

He lay on his stomach on one side of the porch's peak and Davie on the other. His friend had a huge grin on his face. "Having fun?" Nick whispered.

"Fuckin' A." Davie looked down at the street. "How long do we stay here?"

"She'll leave in a minute."

"She's going to set the alarm."

Nick chewed the inside of his cheek, thinking. "Shit." He looked over his shoulder down the slope of the porch roof. "How high up are we?"

"Leg breaking height, with my luck."

They heard the front door open, then close and a key turn in the lock. Nick looked at Davie over the roof peak and held his finger to his lips.

Her heels clacked down the walk as she talked unintelligibly on her mobile phone. The 'beeoopoop' of her car unlocking was followed by the engine starting and the car driving away.

Davie pulled himself up and leaned his arms over the peak. "Now what, mate? We're trapped."

"Maybe," said Nick. He slid to the eaves and slowly pushed himself to his knees. A gum tree with spreading branches looked tempting, but just a smidge too far for a safe jump. The rain spout ran down the side of the building, connecting to the spout from the eaves. He tested its rigidity.

"Don't bother, mate. It probably won't hold you and def won't hold me." Davie pivoted on the peak and crabbed down beside his friend. He pointed at the wall. "That latticework. It looks pretty sturdy. Give it a tug."

Nick stood, balancing himself with the downspout from the top of the house and leaned out and grabbed the wooden frame. "Feels solid."

"You won't know until you test it."

Nick looked back at him and smiled. "You're an arsehole." He gave the latticework another firm tug, then swung out over the garden, grabbed lattice with his other hand and scrambled for a toehold or two.

"Looks like you'll make it. Hurry. We're a bit exposed."

He grunted and picked his way down the latticework until he was close to the ground. He jumped to the grass. "Let's go."

The lattice work shook as Davie descended, pulling away from the house just as he jumped the last metre. He hit the ground and rolled, ending up on his back.

"You okay?"

"Did that look cool or no?"

Nick grimaced and shook his head. "Not even close. Let's get the hell out of here." He reached out his hand and helped his friend up. "Enough shit for one day." He turned and came face to chest of who he had to assume was a concerned neighbour.

"Who are you guys?"

Davie stepped forward, smile on his face and hand extended. "D and N Gutter Cleaning. Just finishing off here." He jabbed his thumb over his shoulder. "Ladder fell in the backyard and the gate is locked. We'll return to retrieve it when the family comes home. Can we interest you in a discounted 'neighbours' quote to clean yours?"

The neighbour looked down at Davie's hand, confusion on his face. "Where's your truck?"

Davie looked at Nick, gave him a slight shrug and slowly withdrew his hand.

"Apprentice kid. Sam. Gone to get us some drinks," said Nick. He looked around, then nudged Davie. "Give Sammo a call and tell him we'll meet back at the office. We'll take your car back."

Davie nodded and pulled out his phone. "Sure thing." He smiled at the neighbour. "We should get going. Give us a call if you want us to clean you out."

They both quickstepped to the car. "Good improv, mate," said Nick. He handed Davie his keys. "Let's get the hell out of here."

Nick walked back to the pool with a fresh cup of coffee. Davie had his head buried in his screen, trolling through the information on his laptop. Or more specifically, the information on Slokow's personal computer, remotely.

"Anything?" asked Nick. He sat at the patio table across from him. "At all?"

Davie shook his head. "Taking home around $18k a month. That's after taxes and a healthy contribution to his and her retirement portfolios. Dvorak pays well. Mortgage, two of them. The house we were at and a summer home on the south coast. Car payments. Two reasonably sized credit cards, both paid off monthly."

"And the wife?"

Davie shook his head. "Everything appears joint. There's not a kernel of evidence that points to him involved in any financial swindling scheme." He held up a finger. "Just a sec."

He rattled the keyboard for a few seconds. Emails showed up on his screen. His head popped up and he looked around. "Where's Kirra?"

"What did you find?"

Davie looked around again, then pivoted his laptop to Nick. He leaned on his elbows and interlaced his fingers, his chin resting on his thumbs.

Nick looked at his friend, then pulled the laptop closer. An email was open, from Slokow's personal email address to Andy Goh. It was dated two days before Andy was killed. One day before Andy contacted Nick. "Shit."

He leaned forward and read the email aloud. *"Hey boss, I've done some looking into that cash thing you mentioned the other day. Can't see anything definitive. Something smells off, but I can't put my finger on it. The books look fine but you know, the gut feels off."* Nick sat up a bit straighter and pointed to the next passage on the screen. *"I hesitate to say this, but if there is something going on, it has to be high in the company. Higher than me, or smarter than me. That's a very small population. Again, I hesitate to mention this, and apologies if I'm way off base, but that very small population includes Kirra. Is she capable of this?"*

Nick slowly closed the laptop. "Damn. He called her out. We need to talk to him."

"You think he's right?"

Nick scratched the back of his head. "Kirra is now a legit suspect. Can we even stay here?"

Davie looked at his surroundings. "It's really nice here, mate. I think if we bug out it'll make her suspicious."

CHAPTER NINETEEN

Nick was woken by yelling from the courtyard. He swung his feet to the floor as his door slowly swung open, Davie knocking lightly as he pushed.

"You awake, mate?" Davie poked his head in.

Nick raised his eyebrows and held out his hands. "Obviously. What?"

"You hear that noise?"

"Obviously. What?" He wiped his hands over his head, wincing as he hit the plaster. "I've got to replace this."

"Might have to wait. They're arresting Murphy."

Nick groaned and stood. Pulled on his shorts and a t-shirt. "He didn't do it."

The yelling continued, the words more distinct.

"Git yer bloody hands off me, ya bloody bell-end," yelled Murphy.

Nick padded out to the front door where two uniforms were attempting to corral Mike into the back seat of a marked car.

Wallace and Lin were standing to one side, watching with amusement on their faces.

Nick marched over. "What the hell?"

Wallace looked at him and closed his eyes in thought. He shook his head. "Have we met?"

Nick pointed at the two uniforms struggling with the smaller but obviously stronger Mike. "Are you guys off your nut? This is the head of security for this house."

Wallace chuckled. "We just popped by to ask some questions, invite him down to the station for a more thorough discussion. He didn't need to arc up like that." He cleared his throat. "Wasn't planning on detaining him, but can't stand for this kind of behaviour. Stay out of our way, son. Best not get your nose in the middle of this."

"This is bullshit."

Lin looked at Nick's head. "Are you okay?"

He reflexively put his hand on the plaster. "Yeah. Fine."

"It's seeping."

He pulled his hand away and looked at the slime of partially congealed blood on the palm of his hand. "Shit." He sighed and looked at Murphy being folded into the back seat. "You're wrong with this guy. I've got to go replace this thing on my head."

"You've known Mr Murphy for a long time?" asked Wallace.

"A couple of days. But that's not the poi - "

"A couple of days?" Lin shook her head. "Go replace the plaster, sir. And like my partner said, keep your nose out of it."

The uniforms successfully wedged Murphy into the patrol car. Lin and Wallace got in their unmarked sedan and followed the patrol car off the property.

"Dammit." Nick looked at his hand again and made his way back to the security office to patch his scalp.

Murphy was handcuffed to the rail along the edge of the table in the interrogation room. Wallace and Lin sat across from him.

Wallace flipped open a file folder and looked at the photo on top. Designed for maximum impact, it was a close up of Andy Goh's bashed in head, malformed and bloody.

He spun the photo around and slid it across the table, expertly weighted so it stopped directly in front of Murphy's face. "Why'd you do this to your boss?"

"Lawyer."

Wallace looked at Lin, who shrugged.

"He said he's on his way," said Lin. "Might be an hour or so."

Wallace leaned close to his partner. "But I don't want to wait, Lin. Time is of the essence."

She shook her head. "We can't force him to talk."

"He could waive his rights." Wallace took off his suit jacket and hung it on the back of his chair. He paced, rolling up his shirt sleeves. "I could make sure he waives his rights."

Lin chuckled. "You saw Macdonald and Goldberg trying to put him the back of their wagon?" She shook her head and chuckled again. "You're not going to make him do anything."

Wallace stopped pacing and sniffed. He glanced up at the camera in the corner. "Professional Responsibilities team probably wouldn't like what I'd do to this guy anyway." He sat.

"I'll tell you what we know happened. If, during the course of conversation you wish to interject and set me straight with something I may have wrong, we wouldn't stop you from talking."

Murphy leaned forward, his weight on his elbows and his arse off his chair. "Listen you freakishly small person. This is the only time I will talk until my lawyer arrives. I was in the SAS for twenty years. I was held captive by the Iraqis for thirteen days before I escaped and walked my way out to Syria. I have seen hell you couldn't possibly imagine." He sat back down. "I'm very comfortable here. I didn't kill Goh. Talk all you want."

He sat back, as comfortable as he could be with both hands shackled to the table.

Wallace barely waited a breath. "I had no intention of cuffing you. This is on you."

He leaned back in his chair and examined his manicured nails for a minute. "You're head of security." He held up his hand to forestall an answer that probably wasn't going to come. "Head of security. Select security cameras turned off before midnight with your login credentials, and turned on again at 10:30 am, after you murdered him. The location of Mr Goh's death is right in the middle of the blind spot created by those deactivated cameras." He held up a finger. "You're a pro; you're probably wondering what we think the motive is." He glanced at Lin. "We are still working through that, but suspect there's a thing going on between yourself and the lovely missus."

Murphy's face flushed an angry red. He leaned forward, opened his mouth and — nothing. He clenched his jaw muscles, took a deep stabilising breath, and shook his head. He interlaced his fingers together and tried to stare the brain out of Wallace's head.

Wallace's eyes flicked to Murphy's for a second, then back to the folder on the table between them. He turned over the page and exposed a studio shot of Kirra. "You had a thing with her, right?"

Murphy looked at his boss's picture and shook his head slightly. And said nothing.

"I think you and she cooked this up together. You kill him, she gets his money and the two of you live happily ever after. After a respectable period of mourning, of course." He shrugged. "Except you're not that smart. No alibi, cameras turned off at the perfect time." He smiled. "Give it a couple of days and I'll have it all mapped out. Or tell me what happened now, and save us both the hassle."

Murphy flexed his forearms, clenched his fists, then breathed out slowly and relaxed. Paid a lot of attention to his fingernails. He leaned back in his chair.

Lin placed the plaster cast created by Dr Cuttey on the table. "The murder weapon looked like this. A crowbar, most likely. We have a team searching the Goh compound."

"It's not a fucking compound."

Lin waited. "That's all you have to say? The team is searching. I'm pretty sure we'll find the weapon."

Mike shook his head and took a deep breath.

"Nothing?" Wallace closed the folder. "Fine. Stay here. Your lawyer should be here in a couple of hours."

Martin Crowe entered the interrogation room and sat beside Mike. They had the room to themselves. Both Wallace and Lin were back at their desks. "You're in a bit of a tough bind, Mike. Your login deactivated the cameras before the killing and reactivated them after."

"A kid could hack into the camera system. Probably did. I wouldn't be stupid enough to do it myself, would I? First place they looked. Nothing else? No physical evidence? Did they find the weapon yet? What's my motive?" Mike threw himself back in the seat. "Lazy cops. Is it because I'm Irish?"

"How about you take a deep, calming breath and don't talk at all when they come back in. I'll take it from here."

"How deep did I bury myself."

Marty smiled and drummed his fingers on the table. "We'll see."

Wallace and Lin re-entered the interrogation room.

Lin glanced at him then looked briefly at Wallace. "We believe we have sufficient evidence to make a case. It'll be the Public Prosecutor's decision whether they will proceed or not. Given the visibility the victim had in Australian business, and he an immigrant himself, I doubt that they'll decline to prosecute."

Mike leaned back in his chair.

"Nothing?"

"Speak to me, not my client," said Marty.

"That's fine. I'll talk, you listen." She slid a sheet of paper across the table to Mike. "All that code stuff shows that you logged in –"

"You showed me this already."

"You said he wouldn't talk." She pulled the sheet back and replaced it in the folder. "There was a fire outside the wall of the compound prior to Mr Goh's murder." She held up a type-written report. "You mentioned that to us on the morning of. That VW was bought by you a week prior, but not registered. You failed to mention that." She extracted another sheet from the folder.

"We found accelerant in your security office that could have been used to start that fire. A great distraction. While the rest of your security team works the fire, you slip back in and kill Goh."

Mike opened his mouth to say something, then shook his head and shut his mouth.

"Admirable restraint, Mike." Marty leaned forward, his hands splayed on the table. "You have no motive and no murder weapon."

She slid the papers back into the folder and closed it. "We believe we have enough. Your client is under arrest for the murder of Andrew Goh and will be held until trial." She stood. "I'll allow you some time to confer with your client."

Martin pulled a tri-folded sheet of paper from his inside suit pocket. "He's coming home with me." He tossed the paper on the table. "Undo his cuffs."

Lin held up a finger while she read the paper. "Pre-trial release?"

"Jesus, Marty. You've had that piece of paper all this time and you don't pull it out until now?" Mike raised his wrists. "The cuffs, please?"

"Cool your jets. Mr Murphy gets some jewellery before he leaves." She sent a message on her phone and placed it face down on the table.

"The cuffs come off when the monitoring bracelet goes on."

"Marty, you agreed to this?" asked Mike

"That, or you spend the next couple of months in a cell while they try cobbling together a case against you."

A technician entered the room with a laptop, and a monitoring bracelet in a case. He placed the case on the table and took out what looked like an oversized digital watch. "Left or right?"

"Doesn't matter."

"Right, then."

Mike smiled and lifted his left foot onto the table. "Do your worst."

The tech strapped the monitoring bracelet to Mike's ankle. He opened his laptop and entered a command. A green LED on the bracelet turned on with a muted beep. "It's activated. You've got an hour to get back to your residence. The property coordinates are the limits of your world until this comes off. Your location is automatically checked every 45 seconds. If you are located outside of the proscribed area, police will be dispatched to arrest you, remove the monitoring device, and place you back in custody. There are no warnings."

"Yeah, yeah. I get it." He rattled the chains. "The cuffs, please?"

Nick looked up from his laptop as Mike entered the pool area. "Hey, you're out."

"Bail. Kirra is very generous. Thanks for hanging around. We need to talk."

Nick slowly closed his laptop. "I'm up to my neck in this money thing she's got us working on."

Mike looked around. "Where's your friend?"

Nick cleared his throat. "What is it you want me to do?"

"What do you think, mate? My taxes. Jesus. I've been accused — arrested — for the murder of my boss, a man I've known and loved for decades. Absolutely ridiculous. And I think you think that, too. I want you to find out who actually killed him." He jabbed a finger at Nick. "And only an idiot would think his death isn't related to the missing money."

Nick nodded. "And I'm not an idiot. It crossed my mind. I am busy, but I'll do what I can. Can you help?"

Mike raised his trousers' leg and showed Nick the monitoring bracelet was strapped to his ankle. "Only within the confines of this property. I leave, the light turns red and I spend the rest of my time, at least until the trial, behind bars."

"At least until the trial?"

"They don't have a case. Extremely circumstantial evidence."

"Do you know how many people are living in Long Bay just on circumstantial evidence?"

Mike sighed. "Don't cheer me up so much, mate. You'll help?"

"I'll do what I can."

"I'll pay you what I can."

CHAPTER TWENTY

Nick waited until Mike had left the pool area. He opened his laptop and entered his personal password. Kirra's emails were on the screen. He opened his messenger app and pinged Davie. *Whatever you're doing, meet me at the pool. Things are changing. Sands are shifting. Some other appropriate metaphor.*

He returned to Kirra's emails. He'd gone back over a month's worth and there was nothing in there that would hint at even a whisper of impropriety. Dead end.

Davie walked onto the pool deck, his laptop under his arm. "What the fuck, man. I was sleeping. 'Sands are shifting'? What kind of shit movies have you been watching?"

"Mike just hired us. Well, me. But I'm hiring you."

"He's still in trouble, is he?"

"Bailed. Ankle bracelet and up against the wall. He makes a good point that Andy's death and the missing money are linked. Stupid not to think so." He took a breath and thought for a second. "I've got to go talk to Slokow about that email. Can you start looking at the killing? See if there's something in the log files for the security system that contradicts the established facts."

Davie smiled. "Cool. This is getting interesting." He sat across from Nick and opened his laptop. "How's it going with you? The money thing."

Nick sighed and tugged an earlobe. "It's like I can smell the dead rodent, but I can't find it. I've tried Benford and Zipf, but the transactional volume really isn't large enough. And even with the marginally small dataset, nothing stands out."

Davie stared at his friend for a beat. "Yeah, I have no idea what you just said."

"Benford's law dictates the frequency distribution of leading digits. Works, progressively less successfully, for second and third digits. Zipf is a similar concept. But I need a significant volume of data for the results to be meaningful."

Davie chuckled and shook his head. "Like that helped any."

Nick slapped his laptop closed and tucked it under his arm. "I'm going to talk to Slokow. Let me know if you find anything on the logs."

"What the hell do you need now, Mick?"

Nick eased into the chair across from Brent Slokow's desk and placed his laptop case on the desk between them. "It's Nick, actually." Slokow was facing three quarters to Nick, reading through some compliance documents on his monitor. "But you know that."

"Whatever. I'm busy. I need to make sure all of our regulatory ducks are in a row before the auditors arrive.."

"Understood. This will only a take a couple of minutes. It's about Kirra, and the missing funds."

Brent pushed back from his monitor and leaned on the desk, fingers interlaced. He spotted the plaster on Nick's head. "What in the hell happened to you?"

Nicked gently touched the plaster. "Cut myself shaving. Tell me what you found out about the missing money."

Brent shook his head. "I could not definitively prove there was any missing money. Did you?"

Nick grimaced. "Something stinks, but I can't find the source."

"Absolutely no use to me." He turned back to his monitor. "Really busy."

"I'm actually here to talk to you about the email you sent to Andy a couple of nights before he was killed."

That stopped Brent. He slowly turned back to Nick. "What?"

Nick shrugged. "It's my job. I'm investigating this. Kirra has given me pretty broad latitude. I'd be slack if I didn't discover that email. What did you mean by it? You said something like if something was going on it had to be someone higher in the company. Few are higher or smarter than you, or something along those lines. Weren't you concerned that maybe Andy was behind this?"

Brent pulled at his lower lip, thinking. "What else have you discovered?"

"I tried the Benford and Zipf tests, to no avail. The numbers seem to look okay from a balance sheet point of view, but there's almost a step change downward in profits from almost a year ago. Eleven months, to be exact. A small dip, but pervasive. Nothing else seems to change, and I can't pinpoint where it happens."

"Benford and Zipf? Haven't even thought about those for years. Nothing at all from them?"

"Too few samples, I think."

Brent nodded. "Probably right. We're still too small."

Nick chuckled. "Too small. Right."

"For that analysis, yeah. Limited product and inventory choices. If this company made internal combustion engines, yeah, but EVs have far fewer parts. Wheels, body, electric motor, drive train, brakes and batteries. A couple of other bobs and bits. Great for inventory control, makes it harder to do what you tried to do."

"You got anything for me? What made you think something was wrong?"

Brent frowned. Shook his head. "I'm not convinced there *is* anything wrong. Goh had a gut feeling. Have you eliminated me?"

"You?" Nick scratched the back of his neck. "This is a bit embarrassing. We've checked you and your wife's financials. Not a hint of anything. Sorry for the prying, I've got a job to do."

"Then check the financials of everyone. Jesus. If you're prying into my personal life, why stop there?"

"Mate, don't be pissed. I was hired by Kirra to investigate this."

"Yeah. And have you investigated her?"

Nick nodded. He slid a notebook out of his laptop case. "We're in the process.."

"We?"

"I've got an IT guy working with me."

Brent placed his hands palm down on the desk and slowly stood. "Serious mistake, Mick."

"Nick."

"You've got a stranger going through the financial background of all the senior employees? What keeps this IT person from publicising what they know? Big mistake, and I'll hold you personally responsible for public exposure of any Dvorak employee's private information."

Nick closed the notebook and slapped it on the table. "I trust Davie. Help me out here. You've done some work already. We know you're not in on whatever it is and I don't want to re-invent the wheel. You care about this company or what? This keeps up it'll get worse and worse until the company is bankrupt."

"Not likely."

"You willing to bet that? Look, I'm doing this. The faster I get it sorted out, the better for all of us."

Brent sighed and sat back at his desk. "Seriously, I need to finish the audit prep. I'll give you what I've already done. You can pull from it what you want. I found nothing." He opened a desk drawer and pulled out a thick file and dropped it on his desk.

Nick lifted it. It was six centimetres thick, and heavy. "You, um, have a digital copy?"

"No."

Nick waited for some, any, elaboration. None was forthcoming. Brent returned to the compliance documents.

"Okay, then." He hoisted the thick file and placed it on top of his laptop case. "I'll scan this and get it back to you."

"No. Jesus, for a supposedly smart guy, you're pretty stupid. If someone is ripping off this company they're a computer whiz. You put anything of your investigation on a computer, anywhere, assume the perp — that's what you call them, right? — assume they have copies. And if you're lucky, they haven't manipulated the info." He looked at Nick. "Don't even copy it. Copy machines are all connected to the intranet." He shook his head. "Idiot."

Nick grimaced and stuck the file and his laptop under his arm while he dug out his phone and called Davie.

"Getting anywhere?"

"Air gap your laptop. Completely. At least the one you've stored any case info on."

"Yeah, duh. Wait, didn't you?"

Nick swore. "Get back to the house, if you're not already there. I'll be back in about twenty. We need to reset. I've got everything Slokow had."

"Right. See you shortly."

Nick pocketed his phone and trotted to the lifts, concerned that maybe they'd been doing worse than wasting their time — they'd been telegraphing their activities to whoever killed Andy.

CHAPTER TWENTY-ONE

Mike met Nick at the gate. "What have you found so far?"

"Davie is looking into Andy's murder. I was just catching up with Slokow about the missing money."

Mike's eyes narrowed.

"But that's why I'm back. I'll drop off this stuff and catch up with Davie and then I'll find you, okay? You can walk me through everything you know from when you woke up to when the cops arrived."

Mike nodded. "I'll be in the security office. I'll be expecting you. Don't be long."

"Right-o."

Nick walked with pace back to the pool looking for Davie. He wasn't there. "Shit." He dropped the laptop and Slokow's file on the table and called his mobile.

Davie walked onto the patio, his phone ringing. "Yeah, what?" He spied the file folder. "Slokow's papers?"

"All hardcopies. Nothing digital." Nick paused. "We should be doing the same. Print everything out, add notes by hand. Maybe." He picked up the file and his laptop. "Find out anything with the CCTV logs?" He walked toward his room.

"A side door root login. Not traceable, but it happened just before Mike's two entries. Extremely circumstantial, but it supports his story."

Nick dropped the file folder on his bed, kept the laptop. "It doesn't help. The system is not very secure. A high school kid could hack in. Mike is getting antsy. I told him we'd drop the money problem for a minute and work on his side of things. He's waiting for us."

"Great. Time with the angry Leprechaun. How's your head?"

Nick gingerly touched the plaster, then again with a little more pressure. "Not bad, actually." He peeled the plaster off his scalp and folded in on itself. "That's better."

Mike looked up from a technical manual as Nick and Davie entered his security office. He picked up his coffee from his desk and moved to a small conference table. "Over here."

There were chairs on three sides of the table and a whiteboard on one of the short ends. Mike had taken a chair on one of the long sides. Davie sat across from him.

Nick slid the notebook from his laptop case and stood by the whiteboard. He picked up a marker and drew a horizontal line across the middle of the board. "We need to sort out your timeline for the twelve hours from 11 pm the night before to 11 am the day Andy was killed." He made a tick on the left most edge and wrote '11 pm' below it. He held up the marker, waiting. "Well?"

"There's nothing."

"What were you doing at 11 pm? It's not nothing." prompted Nick.

"Sleeping." He held up his hand. "Just a sec." He opened his phone and scrolled through his calendar. "I had dinner with Andy that night. It went until a bit after 10:30. Which means I would have been in the gym by 11. Until about 11:30. Light workout."

"Okay." Nick wrote 'gym 11-1130' at an angle. He looked at his notes and made a tick and labelled it '1145 pm'.

"I was in the shower at 11:45."

Nick wrote 'root access' at that time stamp. "Somebody accessed the root of the security system at that time. Hid their tracks fairly well, but Davie found it." He added a tick and '1152'. "And this is where you apparently logged in."

"I didn't."

"We know that. Whoever logged in as root made an entry for you at that time." He added another tick at 1201. "And this is when the cameras facing the front and the gate were disabled."

Mike waved at the whiteboard. "I was passed out by then. I crash fast. Especially after I've had a couple of glasses of good red after the workout." He studied the whiteboard. "Not for nothing, it wouldn't take me nine minutes to disable the cameras. Maybe two, at the most."

"The problem," said Davie, "is proving that you were in bed. Were you…with company?"

"Was I sleeping with anyone? No." He pulled out his phone and found the app he was looking for. "Sleep app. Sleep is the most important part of a healthy life. More important than diet or exercise. I record how deep I sleep every night." He opened the sleep chart for the night in question and slid the phone down the table to Nick. "According to this I was deeply asleep by 11:53 and woke up at 5:48. Received a text from one of the night guys. I recall it wasn't a natural waking. There were flames and smoke and a crowd standing around looking at a fire."

Nick took the phone and looked at the chart. "Deep sleeper." He swiped a couple of nights in each direction. "Fairly consistent with the days before and after, but there's nothing here that guarantees this was in your bed, and not someone else's."

Davie held out his hand. "Give that to me."

Nick slid the phone back up the table. "What?"

"These things have GPS." He looked at Mike. "You mind if I do some expert level prying in your phone? The GPS is tracked continuously, but I need to get into internal registers to find it."

"Will you damage it?"

"Hopefully not."

"Hopefully?" Mike held out his hand. "Give it back."

Davie hesitated. "But I might be able to prove it was in your bed."

"Yeah. Great. I need to back it up first in case you brick it." He closed the apps and opened the settings. "Backing it up to the cloud. It'll take a couple of minutes. Why hopefully?"

"There's an even chance you end up with nothing more than a paperweight when I'm done. I'm good, but the boys and girls in Cupertino are much, much better."

Mike slid the phone back. "Don't make me regret this."

Nick tapped the marker on the whiteboard. "What's next?"

"What do you mean?" asked Mike.

"Need to flesh out this timeline. Up at 5:48," Nick made a mark and labelled it, "and then what?"

"Chased the two guys with the bike helmets who I believe started my car on fire."

Davie pulled his attention from the phone. "That was your Beetle?"

Mike nodded. "My project for the next six months. I was planning on restoring it. It's going to take a lot more now. It's gutted."

"You got back to the house by when?"

"A little after 6:45. Andy was dead in the courtyard and the fire department had just arrived. Shit got crazy after that."

Nick took a step back from the whiteboard and took a picture of the time map. "I don't know how much help this will be, but if Davie can pull the internal GPS data, it might help. Some. Fingers crossed."

"Thanks for the pressure, mate," said Davie.

Mike scrubbed his hair with his fingertips. "Do your best kid. Anything you need, ask."

CHAPTER TWENTY-TWO

Nick knocked on the doorframe of Kirra's studio. She was sketching her next piece on a sheet of paper tagged to her easel. She looked over her shoulder at Nick and smiled.

"What's up?"

"I need a few minutes of your time."

She added a flourish to the edge of the sheet and put her charcoal on the easel. "Sure. I have a few minutes. What's on your mind?"

Nick sighed. "This is a bit awkward."

Kirra sat behind her desk and motioned for Nick to take a seat across from her. "Spill it."

"I met with Brent today."

"What does he have to say for himself?"

Nick squirmed in his chair. "I wanted to find out what he'd already done. So I wouldn't be reinventing the wheel." He paused. "During our investigation we found an email he sent to Andy where he suggested that it was possible you," Nick pointed, "were skimming the money from the company." He held up his hands. "I've found nothing that would suggest you had anything to do with this."

"And you won't." Kirra smiled. "I'm not offended. Brent is a pedant. The perfect person to be accountable for compliance. I'd be surprised if he didn't suggest I could be involved." She interlaced her fingers on her desk. "Is that all?"

"Sorry, no. Can you go through the assets of the company with me? I need an experienced eye."

Kirra chuckled. "Brent would be a better resource."

"Brent is, and I quote, 'tied up with compliance stuff'. He wasn't extremely cooperative."

She nodded. "Audit in two weeks. Did I mention he was a pedant?" She stood and grabbed her keys from her desk. "To the office."

He expected another one of the Dvorak fleet and was surprised when she unlocked an old boxy Land Rover. "This is a surprise."

"I like sitting up above everybody."

Kirra led Nick to a meeting room and projected her laptop on the large monitor on the meeting room wall. "What are you looking for?"

"I got to thinking that with the limited amount of inventory coming into Dvorak, at least compared to the typical internal combustion production facility, it would be really difficult to spoof the finances. I'd like to have you go through all of the tangible assets on Dvorak's books, one by one, and see if there's anything there that looks out of place."

Kirra raised her eyebrows. "What? That'll take days."

"Ignore manufacturing assets for now — the batteries and wheels and tires and whatever else is used to put the cars together. Looking at machinery, properties, offices, warehouses, that type of thing."

"That narrows it down a bit. Why?"

Nick shrugged. "A hunch." He cleared his throat. "This is just the starting point, though. If nothing comes up from the manufacturing assets we'll need to go deeper."

Kirra checked the time. "I can give you an hour."

"Better than nothing, right? Can we get started?"

Kirra sighed and opened the accounting system and navigated to the assets page. Filtered on equipment. "We'll start with the plant equipment. I'm pretty familiar with it. Andy talked about each new piece of equipment like it was one of his children."

Nick opened his notebook. "Fire away."

Kirra zipped through the battery assembly equipment, the engine and drive train units, and the final assembly plants. There were some variations based on car model, and multiple instances for the various manufacturing facilities. But they were all legit, to the best of Kirra's knowledge.

"I'm not sure I understand why we're doing this. These are static. There's no real feasible way to fudge these large pieces of equipment to siphon cash from the company."

Nick shrugged. "Back to basics. Probably nothing, but it clears my mind. Work up to the hard stuff. I never liked diving into the deep end. A slow, timid walk from the shallow end." He pointed at the screen. "Can we look at real estate now?"

"Whatever floats your boat. I can see why Brent wasn't interested in this. It's going to take forever."

"How much real estate does Dvorak own?"

"Very little. Most of it is leased." She waggled her hand. "There's a few properties when you include the charging stations, warehouses, sales centres, service centres."

Kirra navigated to the contracts section and filtered on properties. "This should be fairly quick, comparatively speaking."

A list of properties filled the screen. The top of the list was the head office, a twenty-five year lease, three years in.

"Head office. A beautiful building. Built to our spec and leased to us on a twenty-five year deal."

"Makes sense. You're not a real estate company." He pointed at the monitor. "You've set up over 2500 charging stations?"

"That's for the entire country. There are 2000 charging stations in just Los Angeles alone. A mere 2500 isn't very many for a country this size. We're looking to triple that by the end of the decade."

"Out of curiosity, what kind of revenues do you get from them?"

Kirra smiled, but a puzzled smile. "None, directly. They're free." She laughed at the look on Nick's face. "The more chargers out there, the easier it is to sell an electric vehicle. And we make more than enough profit from the cars to subsidise the charging stations."

"That actually makes sense." The screen rolled to the sales centres. "Not as many of them. The numbers look right to you?"

Kirra quickly scanned the list. Each was tagged with a shopping center. "Yeah. Next."

"Warehouses, then. How does that work?"

"Bulk loading to the main distribution centres, then just in time to the manufacturing facilities. By definition, the main distribution centres are large and near shipping ports — Newcastle, Wollongong, Port Melbourne, Brisbane, Fremantle."

"Just the five of them?"

Kirra stared at the screen. "Yeah. Why are there eight?"

Nick tapped on the table. "That's why we're here." He made a note in his book. "Which three are the extras?"

Kirra highlighted them. All three were in Southwest and Western Sydney "I don't understand. Very few people have the authority to sign leases on behalf of the company." She looked closer at the screen. "And these leases are less than a year old and are for only a year. They expire in two weeks." She looked at Nick. "How does this tie in with missing money?"

"Are they as large as the other three?"

"Based on the lease amounts, I doubt it." She opened the three digital contracts and zipped through them. "As I thought. All three are a tenth of the size, roughly, as the legit ones."

"Leave those open." Nick wrote the address in his book. "The leases expire in a couple of weeks you say?"

"Yes. All three."

Nick finished writing the third address and paused in thought. "Who signed the leases?"

"I'd dig the paper files out of legal archives. Andy or Slokow."

"Do the lease amount account for the decrease in profits?"

Kirra's was shaking her head before Nick finished the question. "Drop in the ocean. It's in the thousands. Not even close to millions." She closed her laptop and disconnected the monitor. "I don't understand. There has to be something else. What's your gut feel for the amount of money pouring out of my company?"

Nick winced. "Somewhere in the neighbourhood of $10 million a quarter." He waggled his hand in a 'so-so' motion. "That's a fuzzy number. Probably on the low end."

"I don't understand how leases on three smallish warehouses can account for that much loss."

"I'm going to grab Davie and check them out. Don't tell anyone about them, okay? We don't want to spook anyone." Nick tucked the notebook into his laptop case. "Can you get the contract info from legal without raising any suspicions?"

Kirra laughed. "I'll see you back at the house."

CHAPTER TWENTY-THREE

"God damn, this is a nice car." Davie ran his hand along the burled teak dash. "Think she'll let you keep it?"

"You're nuts." Nick glanced at the GPS on the dash. "The third one is just around the corner."

"There'll be nobody and nothing there, just like the first two."

Nick rounded the corner and pulled to the curb. The destination was just ahead of them. Three motorcycles were parked by the loading bay. "Recognise those bikes?"

"Oh, Jesus. Let's get out of here."

Nick turned off the car and got out. "I want to see what they're doing."

"You are an idiot. Your head is just getting better." But still he got out of the car and joined Nick. He interlaced his fingers and cracked his knuckles. "Jesus," he said again.

Nick opened the mapping app on his phone and looked at the satellite view of the facility. He zoomed the view from the top of the building. It looked like a set of stairs led up to a landing on the far side of the building. He tapped his phone screen. "There."

Davie cocked his head and looked at the screen. "Probably locked."

"Let's find out."

They arced around the property, coming straight in at the door across a facility parking lot.

"We are wide open, like sitting ducks."

Nick grunted and kept walking. "There's no cameras on the outside, and I doubt those three are sitting around staring out of windows. They're not tall enough. The windows are near the roofline. Keep up."

The quietly climbed the metal stairs to the landing. Nick tested the door. Locked.

"Well I guess that's that," whispered Davie.

Nick slid his lock pick set from his back pocket and squatted in front of the door. "Block me."

Davie slid behind Nick, blocking view from the street. "This going to take long?"

Nick stood and pocketed the kit. "Nope." He turned the knob. "Let's hope maintenance was kept up." He eased the door open. No rusty hinge noises. He smiled and squatted and poked his head in. Stood and motioned Davie to follow.

The landing inside the door was about a metre above the warehouse floor. It wasn't the most attractive piece of real estate Nick had ever seen. The lighting was harsh, provided by a few halogen lights hung from the bare roof.

They cast long dark shadows behind the stack of crates about 20 metres from where Nick and Davie stood. Voices could be heard on the other side.

The walked carefully down the metal stairs to the floor and crept quietly to the crates. The voices on the other side were clearer now.

Davie nudged Nick and leaned close to his ear. "Recognise that voice?" he whispered.

Nick nodded and let out a low growl. "That arsehole. I owe him."

"Hey, hey. There are three of them. Still. Remember how the last time turned out? Let's get out of here."

Nick held up his hand. The talking on the other side of the crates had stopped. "Too late, I think."

The three men came around the corner of the crates.

"Hi guys," said Davie. "Don't suppose we can talk our way out of this?"

The taller of the three shook his head. He wore a dirty T-shirt, denims and square-toed boots, and had an Iron Cross tattoo on his neck. "Persistent little shits, aren't you?" He advanced slowly toward Nick and Davie. "How's the pumpkin, champ? You didn't learn a lesson, did you?"

Nick brushed his hand over the top of his head. "I owe you at least one."

The big guy chuckled. "Hate to do this, really, but there's a lot at stake."

Nick and Davie walked backwards, keeping their distance.

"Why'd you burn the car?"

The tall guy smiled. "No idea what you're talking about."

"What is all this stuff?" asked Nick. He knocked on one of the crates as he backed up. "Label says battery cells. These meant for Dvorak?" He shook his head. "You're stealing battery cells? I thought this was some complicated scheme and it's just a stupid, simple theft?" He laughed. "I'm tearing through the financials, hacking into people's computers, up all night working on this shit and you're stealing bloody batteries? I'm really disappointed."

"Not as disappointed as you're going to be."

"I don't even know your names." Nick and Davie were back-pedalling pretty fast now. "Huey, Dewey and Louie?"

"Snap, Crackle and Pop, I think," said Davie. "Snap is pretty big. You take him and I'll try out Crackle and Pop."

Snap laughed. "This is going to be over so fast."

Davie turned. "Run, Nick."

Nick sprinted after his large friend. "Good idea."

Davie made it to the door and clattered down the stairs on the outside. Nick was a step from the door when he was caught from behind. Someone grabbed his legs and he fell forward. He managed to get his arms up in front of his face before he hit. He felt something go in his left forearm.

He twisted to his back. 'Snap' had him by the ankles and was dragging him onto the floor. He tried kicking, but Snap was too strong. "Come on, man. This isn't going to end well for you."

Snap chuckled. "Definitely not going to end well for you and your friend." He let go of Nick's legs. "Your nose usually get you into a lot of trouble?"

Nick lashed out and tried to kick Snap's lower leg. He missed and as Snap backed up Nick rolled to his knees and scrabbled to his feet, favouring his left arm. He turned and backed against the crates. "Whoa, big guy. Theft will get you in a little bit of trouble, but killing us will put you in Long Reef for the rest of your life."

Snap laughed, slowly advancing on Nick. "If they catch me. And they won't. Our tracks are covered pretty well."

"Who's helping you on the inside?"

Snap swung a fist at Nick who ducked out of the way. The wayward fist connected with the crate, splintering the wood. Nick danced out of the way and ran for the open loading dock door.

Davie ran in front of the loading bay door as Nick reached it. "Move it, mate. These guys aren't screwing around."

The loading bay was about a metre above the road. As Davie ran to the left Nick saw his two pursuers gaining on him coming in from the right. He grimaced. "I'm going to regret this."

He timed his run to catch the one running in front, either Crackle or Pop. Didn't matter which. They both needed to be stopped. He launched himself, spread eagle, misjudging the timing by a split second. He flew between the two, missing them both with the bulk of his weight, but catching them both with his forearms.

That was enough to knock them off their feet, but not enough to cause injury. Not the kind of injury Nick sustained. His hands hit the ground first. Specifically his left hand. The forearm finished breaking with an audible snap. "Son of a bitch!"

He skidded along the pavement, his broken arm pinned under his body. Crackle and Pop rolled to their feet laughing.

Nick rolled on to his back cradling his arm. Crackle and Pop were advancing on him. Davie had stopped running away and was coming back to help him.

Snap jumped off the loading dock, a length of pipe in his hand. "We're finishing this now, kids." He raised his arm to strike Nick.

Davie crash tackled him and drove him sideways, the swing missing Nick, and the pipe clattering across the asphalt. Snap attempted to stand while Davie kneed him in the ribs.

Snap grabbed Davie's leg and flipped him on his back. "You guys never seem to learn." He kicked Davie in the ribs. "Boys, finish Nick off and help me with this lard arse when you're done."

Nick was curled in the foetal position, protecting his head and neck with his right arm, his left arm cradled against his body. Kicks pummelled his body. Someone tried to lift him by his arm, but he pulled it free and tried to scramble away.

The loud roar of a diesel engine drowned out the yelling and screaming and kicking as it swung into the warehouse's loading area. The front fender of a Land Rover glanced off Snap's torso, sending him tumbling across the ground. Crackle and Pop grabbed him and ran to their motorcycles..

The driver's window rolled down. "Get in the truck," yelled Kirra.

Davie helped Nick into the back seat and pulled the door shut. "He needs to get this arm looked at."

Kirra looked at the warehouse, then grimaced and nodded. "Ok. Buckle up. I'll come back here after."

Nick struggled to a seated position. "Kirra, stop at my place. I've got a job for Davie that has to be done right now."

Davie smiled. "How about you give me your keys and tell me what you want, I take the nice car, and you and Kirra go straight to the hospital?"

'Snap' pulled to the side of the road. His two friends stopped behind them. He pulled off his helmet and made a phone call.

"I'm at work, Walter. Why are you calling me?"

"The place has been compromised. I'll arrange to have the inventory shifted, but that space is burned. You should cover all traces."

"Shit. The leases expire in two weeks. Would have been clear."

"I'm moving everything to the first location. It's been months since we used it. It should be clear."

"We wait until dark to move the inventory. We're going to need to put in long hours to complete this."

Walter nodded. "Last one. No point getting sloppy now. Stop by the place tonight and help. You're not going to be getting much sleep for the next couple of days."

"What happened?"

"Your friend and his chubby buddy showed up. I don't know how they found out about the place. It wasn't coincidence."

"You hurt them, I hope."

Walter rubbed his bruised ribs where Kirra's SUV hit him. "Yeah. They're out of the picture for now." He cleared his throat. "But not forever. Is there anything you can do?"

"Jesus, mate. Why am I always having to go around and clean up after you?"

Walter looked at his phone, the call now disconnected. "What a fucking bitch. Let's go, lads."

CHAPTER TWENTY-FOUR

Davie lifted the backpack off his shoulder and placed it on the window sill. He was balanced precariously on a stack of plastic 200 litre drums, stabilising himself with one hand against the wall. "Nick owes me, that prick." He dug in the backpack and removed a wireless camera. Slid the small switch on the bottom to the 'On' position. Leaned against the wall for balance and placed it in the corner of the window frame, pointed at the centre of the warehouse. He'd placed six in windows at the first of the two remaining warehouses, and this was the last one in a window frame for this place.

He made sure it was stable, then opened his phone and checked the monitoring app. All six cameras in this array were lit green. He tapped the icon for the one he'd just installed and the picture was displayed on his phone.

"Good. Now how in the hell do I get down from here?"

Back on the ground he stood in the middle of the warehouse and looked for his installations. Some were visible if he knew where to look, but that was common for most installations. Most people didn't know where to look.

Fortunately.

He slipped his now mostly empty backpack over one shoulder and jogged to the jimmied window he'd crawled through. Exited the way he came in. Closed the window and scattered some dirt on the exterior sill. He stood back and admired his handiwork. Couldn't tell he'd been there.

He turned and looked at his ride. Smiled and brushed dust off his trousers, then slid into the Dvorak convertible and headed back to Kirra's house.

Nick exited the treatment room with his left arm in a cast. It was held snug to his body in a sling. He spotted Kirra, reading a magazine in the waiting room, surrounded by the very best of downtown society, and angled toward her. "Thanks for waiting. You didn't have to. I could Uber back."

She stood and dropped the magazine on her seat. The old woman sitting beside her grabbed it almost before it landed. "What's the verdict?" asked Kirra.

"Bruised ribs, nothing cracked, thank goodness. Non-compound fracture of both bones in my forearm. Set and cast. And I'm on some pretty terrific opiates right now." He took off the sling and dropped it on the chair. Held out his broken arm. "Want to sign it?"

"You're a bit loopy. Let's get out of here."

"Won't argue with that." He blinked and licked his lips. "Dry, too.

Do you have any water?"

"I've got a bottle in the car. Look, I didn't ask much about this on the way here because you were, to put it mildly, in a fair bit of pain." She held open the passenger door of her truck for him. "What exactly happened there?"

"How did you find us? We'd be dead if you hadn't shown up when you did."

She closed the door for him and got in the divers' side. "You first."

He cleared his throat. "Those three small warehouses had to be for something. Smaller than typical, single year leases, something was wrong." He adjusted in his seat, wincing when he absent-mindedly used his broken arm. "Shit. So, the first two we checked were open and empty." He waggled his good hand. "Open in that the windows weren't locked. The doors were, but I don't think it would be that hard to breach them. Definitely not secure. The third one, where you found us, was a different story."

"No kidding."

"We pulled up and saw the three motorcycles owned by the guys who cracked my skull in the alley. That forced a modification to our approach. We — I — picked the lock and found crates of battery cells destined for you guys."

"Are you sure?"

Nick nodded. "Absolutely. They're stealing them."

"And doing what with them?"

Nick shrugged. "Selling them to another manufacturer?"

"There are no other EV manufacturers in Australia. And we order parts to match production, plus a small percentage for spares inventory." She shook her head. "We'd notice if we were missing the volumes. It's more than just theft."

"Then what?"

"I'm not sure. Won't matter much. I'll contact the police when we get home. They can finish this."

"No, no, no. Think about it. You're right. Stealing them when there's no way to on-sell them in Australia doesn't make sense. They're heavy. Shipping them out of the country would be very expensive. And if doesn't justify killing your husband. Sorry. Leave them alone for a couple of days. Davie and I are working on something. Might be able to figure out what the hell they were doing."

Kirra nodded. They reached the gate. Before she had a chance to enter the code the gate started rolling open. Mike stood in the middle of the drive, his arms crossed.

"He looks pissed," said Nick.

"He always looks like that." She leaned her head out of the window. "Outta the way, Murphy, or I'll run you over."

He gave her a half grin and slowly backed out of the way, to the passenger side of the truck. "Nickie, lad. Any closer to getting me out of this bloody ankle bracelet?"

Nick looked down at Mike's leg. The bracelet was covered by his trousers. "Uh, yeah. Closing in on it. A couple more days, max."

"Sure hope so, kiddo." He stepped back. "Your tubby buddy is back. Who said he could drive that car?"

Nick nodded toward Kirra. Mike rolled his eyes and waved them on.

"You better have a way to get him out of that cute piece of jewellery," said Kirra, "or he's going to be really pissed." She smiled. "You'll want to avoid that."

She parked. "What's next?"

"You didn't tell me how you found us."

"I was checking out those three addresses. That was the second one I got to."

"Thank god you were driving the truck. That big guy would bend one of the electric cars."

She put the truck in Park and turned off the ignition. "So, what's next?"

"I need to talk to Davie about that. I've got some ideas, but I need to flesh them out first." He reached across his body to open the car door with his right hand. "This is going to be a pain in the arse."

Davie was at the pool-side table. He looked up when Nick entered. "Sweet, sweet ride, man. I need to win the lottery." He spotted the cast. "Hey, let me sign that thing. Does it hurt?"

"First, no, you'll just draw a dick on it and second, not yet, but the good drugs are wearing off. It will soon." He sat across from his friend. "How'd it go?"

"As expected. Everything is installed. Four nets. The batteries should last a week. We'll see something soon."

"Yeah, I've got some ideas about that. I think I can get closer than just video."

Davie raised his eyebrows and laughed in disbelief. "They tried to kill you this afternoon. How much closer do you want to get?"

Nick took a deep breath. Winced at the pain from his bruised ribs. "Those three apes are just that, apes. They aren't the brains."

Davie leaned forward. "Who?"

Nick hesitated. "Who, what?"

"Who's pulling the strings?"

"You focus on helping Mike with whatever digital sleuthing you need to do. Stay away from these guys."

Walter signalled the truck backing to the loading bay to slow down as it approached. He tapped the side when it had backed far enough. "That's good."

Sam stood beside him. She looked at her watch. "Get this completed before midnight."

"You're crazy. 4:00 a.m. if we're *really* lucky." He pointed at the stacks of crates. "I'm not fucking Harry Potter. I don't have a magic wand. They're heavy and fragile. We're not going to rush this." He looked at her. "Why midnight? You have a date?"

Sam sighed. "Just get it done tonight. Message me when you're finished. I don't care what time it is." She looked at the time again. "Absolutely needs to be finished tonight."

CHAPTER TWENTY-FIVE

Nick tapped the patio table and nodded at Davie. "I'm going to crash." He tentatively touched the scab forming on his scalp. "This seems quaint, now. A bit of a crack on the head. Things escalated pretty fast."

"Speak for yourself. I'm fine."

Nick snorted. "Your ribs are all bruised to shit." He chuckled. "I didn't think you could move that fast, mate. Can you help me tape a bag around my cast? I need a shower. It's been a rough day."

Walter loaded another two crates of battery cells on the hand cart. "My god, this is killing me."

One of his colleagues, recently finished with his load, leaned on his hand cart. "I'm dead."

"Think of the money, Alan. We're making a killing."

Alan wiped sweat from his brow with his sleeve. "Killing. Yeah." He trudged toward the diminishing pile of crates. "I'm going to be dead before we're finished here."

"Suck it up. We need to unload at the destination."

Alan loaded more battery cells on the hand cart. "I hate you."

"Think of the money. Last run. Maximum effort."

Nick lay on his bed, fully dressed, right hand behind his head, left arm in a cast across his stomach. He closed his eyes, running through all of the scenarios.

He opened them and sat up. He sent a text message to Kirra's phone. *We need to talk. U up?*

He sat looking at his phone for a minute before she responded. *Come to the kitchen.*

He swung his legs to the floor and wiped his hand over his face. It had been years since he was this nervous.

He found the kitchen and grabbed a beer out of the fridge.

"You sure you should be drinking that?"

He twisted off the cap and sat in a stool at the kitchen island. "Stopped taking the really good pain meds. Don't need another addiction."

"Another?" She held up her hands. "No, not relevant. What do you want to talk about?"

Sam was also wide awake in bed. She checked the time. "Dammit." She grabbed her phone from the bedside table and called.

"I said we'd be finished by 4:00. There's still two hours to go."

"Shut up, Walter." Sam swung her feet to the floor. "I need to know how the place was compromised."

"Water under the bridge, Sam. We've got work to do and if you're not here to help us, get off the phone and let me get to it."

"Don't pretend you're the brains of this gig, Wally. How?" She grabbed her shorts off the floor and pulled them on, phone jammed between her shoulder and her chin.

"How, who knows? That Nick chump and that other fat arse are better than you clearly think they are."

Sam sat hard on the bed. "How did Nick find out?"

"He's an annoying little gnat. I wouldn't worry about it too much."

Sam thought for a minute.

"You there?" asked Walter.

"Yeah, yeah. How much have you loaded onto the truck?"

"About two thirds. Why?"

"I think I know the 'how'." She pulled her shirt off the bedpost and struggled it on. "And if he found that one, he knows about the other two. Are there *any* other warehouses we can use? Not on the books?"

Walter snorted. "Yeah, I've got four in my other pants. Are you kidding?"

"The risk has reached levels I'm not comfortable with. We should abandon."

"That's nuts. Six, seven million, just thrown away? No. You don't want to do this, you'll owe the rest of us the cut we would normally be getting. Out of your pocket."

"That's not how this works."

"If we didn't need you to do this, we'd do it on our own. We don't have that luxury. But I'm getting my share for this load, one way or another."

She scrubbed her hair with her fingertips. "Okay, dammit, I'm going to regret this. You need to beef up security at the second place. And we need to pull the schedule forward. Get this done and into the system quick."

"What are you going to do about Nick?"

"He's smarter than I remember him to be."

"You know him?"

"From a long while ago." She sighed. "I'll handle him. Keep your friends close and enemies closer, right? I'll think of something."

"What do you mean?"

"Get back to it. I'll be there in a few."

CHAPTER TWENTY-SIX

Nick rushed Davie through his breakfast.

"What's this about?" Davie stuffed his laptop into its case. "Am I going to need this?"

"I don't know." He showed Davie his phone. "I just got a text from Kirra that we both need to meet her at the office ASAP. Bring your laptop. Who knows?"

"Okay. Another ride in the nice car."

Kirra met them at reception. She motioned for them to follow her. "I've got a room on 10."

They tailgated her through the access doors to the internal stairwell and down three flights. As they walked past Sam's cubicle Nick looked in. She wasn't there. He frowned and followed Kirra and Davie into the small conference room. Kirra stood on one side of the small table, frown on her face, Davie sat on the other side. Nick slid his laptop onto the table and sat beside Davie.

"What's up, Kirra?" asked Nick.

She paced. Shook her head. "I'm concerned about how this is playing out." She looked at Nick's cast. "Very concerned. We don't seem to have come to any definitive conclusion and I've spent thousands of dollars."

Davie held up a finger. "Hang on. We found the theft of those battery cells. That's something, right?"

"It's not evidence of underlying internal fraud. It's theft. The police will handle it."

"I don't - I don't think that's good idea, Kirra," said Nick. "A really bad idea. That's just the tip of the iceberg."

"Whatever it is, we – I – can stop it now. Thanks for your efforts and goodbye."

Nick cocked his head and looked at Kirra, trying to read her thoughts. "What else is going on?

She gestured at Nick's broken arm, "you're a liability. You didn't sue the company this time, but there's no telling what you might do if something else happens to you while you're," she used air quotes, "'on the case'."

"Horse shit."

Davie opened his mouth to interrupt and Nick held up his hands. "No, Davie, this is bullshit." He pointed accusingly at Kirra. "I think we're getting too close to what's really going on and she's in the middle of it. So, clearly, she's firing us."

"That's bullshit, and you know it," said Kirra.

Nick shrugged. "How will I ever know if you fire me?" He pushed his chair back. Levelled his finger at Kirra. "If my day rate isn't deposited in my account by close of business I'll see you in court." He grabbed his laptop case. "Let's go, Davie."

"Leave the car keys on the table. And Davie, you stay for a minute."

Davie looked confused, alternating between Kirra and Nick. "I - I don't know."

Nick nodded and dropped the Dvorak key fob on the table.. "Sure. Whatever." He yanked the meeting room door open. Sam was sitting across the walkway at her desk.

She glanced up at Nick. "You're having a bad day. What happened to your arm?"

"Slipped." He kept walking.

"You just got fired?"

He stopped walking. "Mutual agreement."

"That's not what it sounded like from out here."

Nick sighed and kept walking.

Sam waited until Nick was at the lift lobby and made a call. "Walter, how's the repackaging going?"

"The truck's unloaded. This place is covered in dust. We're three hours into what is probably going to be a thirty hour job. The other two are resting for a couple of hours. Last night was murder."

"I think the pressure is off. Nick was just fired."

"How do you know?"

"They were in the meeting room across from my cube."

"In earshot of you?"

"Not for the first part of the meeting, but I got back as it was ending. He's pissed, and so was Kirra." Sam looked at the meeting room. "Hang on, the chubby friend is still in there with her. Maybe Nick was fired but the friend is still on the job." She shook her head. "Okay. The pressure isn't off. But I've got an idea."

Davie was still very confused. "What's going on?"

"Despite what Nick believes, I'm not part of whatever this scheme is. You're smart with computers, please keep digging. And if you can find out how Mike was framed for Andy's murder, that too."

"I know nothing about financial crimes."

"I don't need you to find financial crimes, I need you to find any computer interactions that don't make sense. I was paying Nick two thou a day. That goes to you, now."

She opened the door and held it for Davie. Scooped the key fob off the table and tossed it at him. He just managed to grab it out of the air.

"Yeah, I'm not sure I can do this for you."

"Oh. Ethical issues?"

"No. Technical. I'm a code nerd. Nick had the creative mind, figuring out where to go in the investigation. I just did what he asked."

"We'll work together on this. I've got to get back to running this company I've inherited. I'll see you at the house tonight."

"Well - "

"Remember, I'm paying you the same amount I paid Nick. Text me your bank details."

"Well, okay then."

Nick tried the gate code three times before acknowledging to himself that it had been changed. He pressed the buzzer at the gate.

Mike's voice scratched out of the speaker. "Where's the car?"

"Why'd you change the access code?"

"Talk to the boss."

"Let me in. I've got to pick up my stuff."

"Where's - never mind. See me before you leave." The gate clattered open wide enough for Nick to enter, stopped, then slowly started closing.

"Shit." Nick darted through the closing gap, twisting sideways and banging his cast on the edge of the gate. "Son of a BITCH."

He went straight to the security office and yanked the door open. "You arsehole. Trying to break my arm again?"

"Shit man. Sorry. Where's the car?"

"I've been fired. Kirra has the keys."

Mike slowly lifted his trousers' leg to expose the monitoring bracelet on his ankle. "I take it you're going to be useless me."

Nick shrugged. "Talk to your boss. Maybe Davie will help. I'm going to grab my stuff and get out of here."

Mike waved him away. "Thanks for nothing, kid."

CHAPTER TWENTY-SEVEN

Nick dumped his belongings in the middle of his living room floor. The lights were back on. There was no food or beer in the fridge and he was hungry. And thirsty.

The return to his piece of shit car was a soul killer. It had an interior smell he hadn't noticed before. The door squealed when he pulled it closed. He started the car, finagled his phone out of his pocket and sent a text message. He reached across with his right hand to put the car into gear.

He stopped at a bottle shop and picked up a slab of beer. Paid one of the employees $10 to put it in the boot of his car. Picked up a lamb and chicken kebab with hot sauce to go and drove back home.

Where he discovered carrying a slab of beer up to his apartment with one broken arm wasn't as hard as he thought it would be.

He twisted the top off a bottle, spread the kebab out on a plate and sat down in front of the TV. "This isn't so bad." He picked at the beer label. "Who am I kidding."

He dragged his laptop onto his lap and sent a short, sharp email.

Don't appreciate you ripping me off like this, Kirra. Kinda suspicious, if you ask me. You still owe me $4k. Pay up or I continue investigating on my own. Nick

He looked at the message for a second, then nodded to himself and sent it. "Take that." He turned on the television and sat back as a footie match played out in front of him. He didn't care who won. Didn't even care who was playing. It was a distraction.

For about three minutes.

His laptop pinged an alert for an incoming email. A reply

I disagree with the amount you say I owe you. I can't stop you from spending your own money investigating, but you're drilling a dry hole. /BR Kirra.

He slapped his laptop closed. Someone had just scored in the game, so he took another drink. Picked at more of his kebab. Sighed and opened his laptop and replied to the email.

I don't need money to sue you. I can get a personal injury lawyer on contingency. I'm sure there'd be a line of them once they find out what you and Dvorak are worth.

Sent.

He opened another bottle. There was a fracas on the screen, but he only gave it a glance. Refreshed his email until he received a response.

If that's your intent I have to insist on no further direct communications. My legal counsel will be in touch with you.

Nick nodded and slowly closed his laptop. "That's that."

He took a large mouthful of kebab just as his phone rang. He grunted as he tried to get the food down his throat so he could talk. "Hang on." He chewed and swallowed and returned to the phone.

"What do you want, Davie?"

"What actually happened today?"

"I got fired. I take it that you staying behind means that you're now on the case?"

"Uh, yeah."

"You get the car?"

Davie chuckled weakly. "Yeah. Nice car."

"Be careful. Probably best if we don't communicate until this is over."

"This? What is this? I thought this was just a battery cell theft."

Nick sighed. "Maybe. Plus there's Andy's murder. You're taking that one too?"

There was a long silence on the phone.

"You still there, Davie?" Nick took another drink of beer.

"Yeah, I should go. I'll buy you a beer once all this is over."

"Sure, mate." He hung up and tipped back the beer, opened a third. He needed that buzz.

He finished the kebab and another beer before he made the call he had to make.

"Sam Epping speaking."

"You don't have my number in your phone?"

"Ah, Nick. How's it feel to be fired when you were so close to solving the riddle?"

"That's what I want to talk to you about. I know it's not just theft. I think I have a pretty good idea what was going on. And if I can figure it out, I'm certain that Kirra can. She's smarter than I am."

"There's a long list of people smarter than you."

"I want to help you pull it off under her nose. I know what she's going to do." Nick suppressed a belch. "And I know where Davie would have placed the cameras in the backup warehouse."

There was a pause. "You -" She paused again. "Cameras?"

"Yes. Very difficult to find, networked back to Davie's laptop."

"Son of a bitch. If I see you again, I cut you." She terminated the call.

Nick looked at his phone debating whether to call her back, then decided against it. Tossed the phone on the sofa beside him and forced himself to a standing position. "This can't end this way," he said, shuffling to the bathroom.

CHAPTER TWENTY-EIGHT

Nick was stretched out on his sofa in a partial stupor, ignoring a game show on his television when someone knocked on his door. He angled his head toward the door. "Later, Davie. We shouldn't talk right now."

The knocking continued.

He groaned and swung his feet to the floor. "Ease up, Davie. You don't want to see me right now. I can't help you."

And again, the knocking.

"Fine." He padded to the front door and peered through the peep hole. Stood up straight when he saw the knocker. "Huh."

He released the deadbolt and opened the door to Sam. "You going to cut me?"

Sam chuckled. "Can I come in?"

"Answer my question first."

"I may have been a bit hasty with that comment. There'll be no cutting by me today." She nodded toward the apartment. "So? You going to let me in, or do we talk out here in the hall?"

He stood to one side and let her enter.

She dropped her bag on the coffee table beside the empty beer bottles and kebab remnants. "Wow. This is a shit hole."

"Why are you here again?"

"You have any more of those beers?"

Nick hesitated, then got one for her out of the fridge.

"You're not drinking with me?"

Nick nodded at the bottles on the coffee table. "I'm good. Why are you here?"

She twisted the top off and gingerly sat on the sofa. "How old is this piece of furniture?"

Nick grabbed the remote and turned off the television. "If I had two good arms I'd throw you out the window. Why. Are. You. Here?"

She sipped her beer then placed the bottle beside the others. "Your 'cameras' comment got my interest. I've told the team to pull back. But I can't hold off for long. Small window to get this done or I lose, well, let's say I'll lose a lot of money."

"A lot?"

"Kirra was paying you, what, $2,000 a day?" She laughed. "Don't look so surprised, Nickie. You're not the only one who can hack. Except I can't really call it hacking, can I?"

He glanced at his laptop and scowled. "Shit."

"And she paid you only for what, two days?" She took another mouthful of beer. "Your suit, if you even find a lawyer to take it, will take years and you probably won't win."

"You sit here drinking my beer and giving me all this great news.

You must be a blast at office parties." Nick dropped in a chair at right angles to Sam. "You're about to lose a bunch of money and why in the hell should I care?"

She cleared her throat. "Fifty thou. That's why you should care."

"For…?"

"Helping me out."

He leaned forward. "How much is your end if you're throwing me that? And more importantly, why should I trust you?"

Sam shook her head. "You don't get to know my end." She looked around. "I'll never have to live in a shit hole like this." She took a sip of beer. "Trust me? That's on you. I don't think we want to set up an escrow account for this sort of thing. Too much paperwork. Too many prying eyes. So, it's on you."

"What's the money for? Keeping quiet? Everyone who needs to know already knows about the battery theft."

"Cameras, mate. You're not paying attention. Find them for me. Disable them. Let us finish off the work tonight. Last job. Forever. But we can't do it with the cameras there. Can't even go in there."

"You're a hacker. Hack them."

"You know as well as I do that hacking into a known, existing network, like the one at Dvorak, is fairly simple. Hacking into an unknown network, well I can do that, but it'll take a few days and I don't have that kind of time. Need to finish this tonight."

Nick took a deep breath. "You're willing to give me – "

"For Christ's sake. Yes. Fifty thou to clear out the cameras. Nothing else." Sam placed her bottle sharply on the coffee table. "No? I can snap that other arm before I leave. You'd like that?"

Nick stood and picked the empty bottle off the coffee table. Dropped it in the recycle bin with a clatter. "Fifty isn't much for the risk I'm taking."

"What risk?"

He collected the remnants of the kebab and wrapped it in the foil it came in. Dropped in the garbage bin and took another beer from the fridge. Twisted off the top and sat in the chair. "I'd be an accessory to whatever crime it is you're committing. And there's no way you're going to get away with this."

"Got a secret for you, Nickie. I've been getting away with this for almost a year. And in two, two and a half weeks the external audit will come up clean and nobody will know it ever happened. As long as I get this finished tonight so the final steps can play out."

"It's really not just a battery theft."

"You said you knew what it was."

"Well, a bit of a bluff. Double it."

"I could stab you right here."

"You'll never find all the cameras. You'll think you found them all, but you'll miss at least one."

"Seventy-five."

"A hundred, or get the fuck out of here."

Sam pursed her lips. "Much as I'd love to break that other arm..." She snapped to her feet. "You know the warehouse. Meet me there in an hour."

"One hundred?"

She nodded.

"I'll be there." Nick watched her leave. "Shit. Which one?"

He opened his laptop and the mapping program. Entered the address of the first place he had visited with Davie. It was in Campbelltown, in southwest Sydney, and more than an hour's drive away. He shook his head and entered the other address. It was in a mixed business/factory area near Parramatta and about a forty-five minute drive away. "That better be it."

Fifty minutes later and Nick rolled to a stop outside the warehouse. Three motorcycles were parked beside the loading bay. He turned off the ignition, got out and leaned against the car. Traffic at the surrounding warehouses was light. It was near the end of the day. He took a deep breath and let it out slowly. "May as well get this started."

He walked up to the loading bay. The three -- Snap, Crackle and Pop as he knew them -- were sitting on the ramp.

Walter stood and clenched his fists. "Lads, the moron is following us." He took a step toward Nick. "Gonna give you three more casts to match that one."

Nick back-pedalled. "Hang on. Ease up. I was invited here by Sam." The two others in Snap's gang followed. "Seriously. Call her. She'll tell you."

"Nice story. You must think we're idiots."

Nick had his right hand up in surrender and his left arm, in a cast, awkwardly replicating the right. "Not at all. Understandable. Completely surprised me, too. I'm just here to get rid of the cameras so you guys can go in."

"She *did* tell us to get out of the warehouse." said Crackle.

"I didn't see any." Snap took another step toward Nick. "I think it's bullshit to throw us off."

Nick scrambled for his phone. "No, really." He opened the network app. "Look." He selected the network with the six cameras in the warehouse he was tasked to remove. The thumbnails were arranged in a grid. "Here."

Walter grabbed the phone from Nick and tapped one of the thumbnails. The video from the camera filled the phone's screen. He grunted and handed the phone back. "She didn't say anything about how many."

Sam walked around the corner with a bag in her hand. "I certainly don't tell you everything, Walter. Nick, get rid of the cameras." She held out the bag. "The rest of you put these balaclavas on while you help him. Keep them on until the cameras are taken care of."

CHAPTER TWENTY-NINE

Davie drove up to the gate at Kirra's house and realised he didn't remember the code to get in. "Shit." He pressed the intercom buzzer and leaned his face close to the camera.

"*You* have the car?"

"Hey, um, Mr Murphy, can you open the gate? What's the code so I don't have to bug you again? I've forgotten it."

"Boss lady knows about all this?"

"Yeah. I'm the point man now." Davie cleared his throat. "I'll do what I can to get to the bottom of Andy's murder, also."

"Mighty generous of you." The screen went blank and the gate started rumbling open.

"So, no to the code, then?" Davie waited until the gate was open enough to pass through then gunned it.

And immediately regretted it. He wrenched the steering wheel hard to the left to avoid hitting the portico and eased to a stop on the lawn. "Dammit dammit dammit". He place it into reverse and backed into the parking spot like that was his intention all along.

He turned off the car, closed his eyes and took a deep breath. Opened the door to come face to face with Mike.

"You don't deserve that car."

Davie shrugged. "Can you get someone to help me with these?" Two monitors in their packaging stuck up out of the back seat. He opened the forward storage compartment and lifted a third out. "There's a bag in the back seat on the floor with cables and splitter boxes. Can you hand it to me?" He grunted and adjusted the monitor he was carrying and snagged the bag. "Thanks. Setting these up in the room Nick was staying in."

"These come from Dvorak?"

"Dvorak's credit card." He smiled. "Kirra's account, actually." He lugged the monitor into the room and made space on the desk for it. He removed everything else off the desk and set up the networking equipment.

Mike dropped the other two monitors on the bed. "What is all this stuff?"

Davie looked up at him briefly then returned to setting up the equipment. "Can you unpack those two? I placed cameras in the two warehouses we believe are being used for some kind of theft. These are to see what the cameras see. CCTV, but better."

"Maybe you're not useless."

"Thanks. I'm not." Davie side-eyed Mike and muttered under his breath. "Wanker."

"What was that?"

"I said 'Thank you'. Can you hand me those monitors?" Davie connected the HDMI cables to the distribution box and connected his laptop. Fired up the monitoring software and selected the first of the four banks of six cameras.

"How are they powered?" Mike pulled up a chair and sat beside Davie.

"Battery. They're in standby mode until a motion detector triggers them. The battery will last 48 live hours. Since we think this is going to go down tonight, that should be more than enough time."

The six squares, two per monitor, were black. "Nothing here," said Mike

Davie nodded. "Third bank, then."

"What about the second?"

Davie smiled. "Before Nick was fired he had a good idea. He knew that they'd have to shift to one of these two warehouses, so we wired them both."

"That's two banks of cameras."

"This is where Nick was smart. One bank of cameras in each warehouse is hidden fairly well, but would be discovered with a decent search. There's a second bank extremely well hidden. Almost impossible to find. That's banks two and four. If bank one isn't live, neither is bank two."

Mike nodded in appreciation. "Bank three then."

Davie entered the command, and all six video panels came to life. "They're at the warehouse near Parramatta."

Five of the six panels showed static pictures of the interior of the warehouse. Various angles of stacks of boxes. Davie pointed at them. "Recognise those?"

Mike tilted his head and looked closely at the image with the largest representation of the boxes. "Those are crates of battery cells we use for our cars. From…" he squinted. "Can't make out the vendor's name. But they're ours." He pointed at the sixth panel. "What's that?"

Davie selected the panel and blew it up to the full monitor size. It was looking out the loading dock door. At the very left edge of the image he could see three men, sitting on the dock with their backs to the camera. One of them significantly larger than the other two. "That's Snap, Crackle and Pop. Ran into them before. That's how Nick's arm got broken." He selected a key and started recording the video.

Mike pushed his chair back. "What's the address? I'll call the authorities and have them picked up and the batteries returned to our distribution centre."

Davie held out a hand. "No, hang on. Kirra and I discussed this, this afternoon. It's more than just battery theft. We're recording so we can let it play out. Don't call the cops."

Mike sighed. "Listen, kid. If this doesn't work I'm going to be really pissed off."

"It'll work. It'll work."

Mike pulled his chair closer to the monitors. "Do you have audio?"

"Just a sec." He tapped a couple of keys and turned up the volume. Hissing came from the speakers. There were voices, but they were distant and not distinct.

"Can you do anything with the audio? I can't make out what they're saying."

"I can do a little bit." Davie launched an audio equaliser program and adjusted the filters until the voices were a little bit clearer.

At that moment a fourth figure appeared approaching the three seated men. Davie leaned forward. "That looks like Nick."

"Is this live?"

"Yeah. Of course." Davie held up his finger and turned up the volume further, The big guy stood and started walking toward Nick,

"Gonna give you three more casts to match that one."

"Oh, shit, this isn't going to end good," said Davie.

Nick said something on screen, but he was too far from the microphones to pick it up.

"What the hell is he doing there? He was fired. Dammit, he's going to get pulverised."

Mike put a hand on his arm. "Quiet. They're still talking."

One of the smaller guys slid off the loading doc. *"She did say there were cameras."*

"She? Who? Kirra?" Mike was standing. "What in the hell is going on here?"

"Sit down, idiot. Sam."

"Who is Sam?"

"IT at Dvorak. Kirra and I think that she's behind this. She and Nick have a history. She told me that's one of the reasons he was fired." He took a deep breath. "I've known the guy for years. I can't imagine he's got anything to do with this, but," he pointed at the monitor, "there he is."

Nick and Snap, Crackle and Pop had moved far enough away from the warehouse to make the microphones useless. Sam moved into frame and started talking, too low to hear. "It looks like Sam is there too. It's happening." She held out a bag and the three men pulled on balaclavas.

The hissing from the speakers filled the room. "Turn off those speakers, mate. The noise is driving me nuts."

CHAPTER THIRTY

Sam led the way into the warehouse. "You're here for one reason, and one reason only. Find the cameras and remove them. Find them, turn them off, disconnect them, and give them to me."

Nick stood in the middle of the warehouse and slowly turned, looking at the light fixtures, the exposed beams, the dirt-filmed windows. A million places to plant a camera. A million places for Davie to plant a camera. And he knew Davie planted twelve of them.

"I'd put four in here to get full coverage. Maybe six if I'm generous."

"What in the hell are you talking about? You put them here," said Sam. "Where are they?"

"I didn't. Davie did. But I know how Davie thinks. I trained him." He held up his cast. "I'm going to need assistance retrieving them, though. Can't climb a ladder with this."

"What in the hell is he doing?" Davie watched Nick as he stood in the middle of the floor, slowly turning. He activated the audio as Nick held up his cast.

"*…need assistance retrieving them, though. Can't climb a ladder with this.*"

Davie held his head in his hands. "He's helping them."

"That's disappointing. Though not surprised, if I'm honest." Mike sat beside him. "There are twelve there?"

"Yeah. These six and the six backups."

Mike nodded at the screens. "Display all twelve."

Davie entered a couple of commands and each of the three monitors were split into four images. Numbers 1 through 12 labelled each image in the upper right hand corner. Nick was motioning to the tall guy who had an extension ladder.

"Walter, right? There's one in the bottom corner of that window.' He pointed. "Obvious once you know where it's at, right?"

Walter steadied the ladder against the wall. "Not climbing this." He turned to the other two. "Barry, go up this damned thing and get the camera."

The man Nick had thought of as Crackle ambled over and looked up at the window. "Where is it?"

Nick pointed with his good arm. "Bottom right corner. See it?"

Barry squinted. "Oh, yeah. How'd I miss that?"

"You were never looking for it, idiot. Get up there and bring it down."

"So 'Snap' is Walter and one of the others is Barry." Davie made a note.

Mike slapped hm on the arm. "Look."

A balaclava'd face got larger as he climbed the ladder. Just when it almost filled the screen his hand covered the camera lens. And the picture turned black.

"One down, eleven to go." Davie checked the time. "It's going to be a long night, I think."

"Turn the sound back off. The hissing is driving me nuts."

Nick held the first camera in his left hand and switched the power off. "One down, five to go." He checked the time. "It's going to be a long night, I think."

"Then step it up, mate. Where are the others?" Walter nodded at Barry. "You work with this arsehole. I've got stuff to do."

Barry struggled to retract the extension ladder. He glared at Nick while he lowered it.

"Hey, mate, I'd help if I could. You're going to want to move the ladder over to the other side, by the third window from the end. I saw another one."

He lugged the ladder to the opposite side of the warehouse. "Shoulda broke your neck."

"Whoa. So hostile." Nick pointed to the window. "Bottom left corner, this time."

He waited while Barry extended the ladder, climbed it and retrieved the camera.

Barry climbed down, stood in front of him, flipped the small switch to the off position and dropped the camera on the floor and smashed it with the heel of his boot. "Where's the next one?"

"That was $300, you twat." Nick scooped up the parts and examined them. Stuck the larger parts in his pocket. "I'll send Sam an invoice."

"Good luck. How many more?" He glanced up at the rafters. "Is that one?"

Nick looked up. Nodded and smiled. "Yeah, I saw that one while you were up the ladder getting the last one. The ladder will be tricky. I'll balance it for you."

Barry glared at him as he extended the ladder to lean against a truss.

"What?" asked Nick. "I'm not going to let you fall. Sam would sic the big guy on me."

"You find the next one while I get this one. And stay away from the ladder."

"Aye, aye, captain." He glanced at the three left for him to find: One opposite the loading bay doors, one opposite the front door and one more in a window.

"Turn the sound back on. I want to listen to them," said Mike.

"Jesus. Make up your bloody mind." Davie entered the command to reactivate the audio. A hiss filled the room.

"It'll do. Where are we at?"

"He's pointed out five cameras so far. Seven to go."

"Jesus, they're slow."

"It took me two hours at each warehouse to install them. It'll take at least that to remove them." Davie pointed at the monitor. Barry's face was filling camera number six, then his hand reached out and grabbed it and for a second there was a vertigo inducing fall as he dropped the camera from the top of the warehouse to the floor.

Then the panel for that camera went black.

"That was uncalled for."

Mike grunted. "Seems like a big waste of money." He rolled his chair away and looked at news on his phone.

"Yeah. About $300 a pop. But we're halfway through."

Davie watched the one called Barry on five of the other six cameras. He didn't show up on the camera facing the loading bay doors. He climbed down the ladder and retracted the extension. He took the ladder and stowed it in the corner and went to join the others. Nick stayed standing in the middle of the warehouse, leaning against a pallet of battery cells. He looked at Sam and her muscle, then up at the camera facing the front door and winked.

"Did you see that?"

Mike rolled his chair over. "What?"

"Just a second." He shut down the network strand with the six disabled cameras and opened a terminal window on the first monitor. Executed a couple of commands and launched a video player. He scrubbed the video forward until Barry was stowing the ladder. He zoomed in on Nick's face. "Look at this."

On camera Nick looked over at Sam, then directly at the camera and winked.

"Son of a bitch. He's still helping Kirra."

Mike scowled. "Was he fired, or not?"

"I think we need to talk to the boss."

CHAPTER THIRTY-ONE

'That's all of them?" asked Sam. She scanned the rafters. "You're not holding out on us, are you?"

"That's the works."

She nodded. "You better not be wrong. Take off the masks and get to work, guys."

Nick started easing toward the door.

Walter chuckled. And grabbed him by his cast. "Get back here. We're not done with you yet."

"Take it easy." Nick pulled his arm free and wiggled his fingers. "I'm still a little pissed off about the broken arm. Don't make it worse."

Walter looked down at him and laughed. "What ya gonna do, champ? Tell your mommy?" He patted Nick on the head, then shoved him toward Sam and the crates. "Because of you, we're a day late. And," he chuckled, "you're no help."

Nick took a good look at what he'd gotten involved with. There were hundreds of crates stacked aimlessly about the warehouse, barely making a dent in the overall floorspace. A hired moving truck was backed to the loading dock.

He shrugged. "I don't get it, Sam. Where are you going to sell these?"

"Shut up, arsehole." Walter pulled Sam aside. "I don't trust him as far as I can throw him. Though I'd like to find out how far I can throw him. Let me scrub this place. No way he told us where all the cameras are."

Mike hung up the phone. "She's leaving the office now. Will be here in about fifteen minutes." He pointed at the monitor. "They're looking for more. How well did you hide the others?"

"Won't survive a really thorough search, but I don't think they have time for that. And really, as long as they leave one we're still good." Davie slumped in his chair. "I should have taken longer to conceal them."

"Can you do anything about it now?"

"No."

"Then shut up the face."

They watched Walter and the other two moving the ladder around and checking windows and rafters for recording devices.

"They're pretty thorough."

Davie smiled. "Haven't come close yet."

"Close to what?"

Davie and Mike turned to greet Kirra.

She pointed at the monitor. "Nick is there?"

"You don't sound shocked," said Davie. "You arranged this with him?"

"You're pretty quick. Nick convinced me that he had to get inside whatever is going on. He knew Sam was in on it, but he's not sure what 'it' is. Either am I."

"There are about three and a half, four thousand batteries in there, Kirra," said Mike. "All of them destined for our Newcastle distribution centre."

"Stupid theft. She can't sell them to anyone. And she'd be really stupid if she tried to sell them back to me." She pulled over a chair and sat. "They got one."

Davie and Mike spun in their chairs to check the monitors. Walter's face filled one of the monitors and his hand grabbed the camera. The image went murky black for a second, then the feed was cut.

"Still five left," said Davie, with a concerned furrow between his eyebrows.

"Four." Another face, another hand, another camera taken offline. Mike stood to leave. "This isn't going to end well, and will do nothing to clear my name. I'm gone. Can't bear watching."

Kirra waited until he left the room. "You know where this is, right?"

Davie nodded. "It's the one near Parramatta."

"I should call the authorities."

"Maybe hang on a second. We're still in the dark about what they're doing with the batteries. They may not get all of them."

She sighed. Stood and paced, returning every couple of circuits to look at the cameras. Nick and Sam were still standing by the loading dock door while the other three searched for the remaining cameras. "They going to find them all?" She shook her head and answered her own question. "They're going to find them all."

Davie ran his fingers through his hair. "You're probably right."

Walter threw another camera to the ground in front of Nick's feet. "That's three. We'll go through this place until we find them all. And we *will* find them all."

Nick picked the pieces off the floor. "Davie was way more thorough than I expected. I'm impressed." He pocketed the remnants. "I'm going to add the cost of these cameras to my invoice, though. They ain't cheap."

"I'm going to break a few dozen bones in your frail body." Walter nodded at Sam. "You're not paying him for — anything, are you?"

"Hundred large, Wally. She's paying for my help." Nick pressed. There were still three cameras active. He needed them to talk.

Sam opened her mouth and Walter jumped in. "No, Sam. He's holding out. You should let me dump him down a sewer drain." He stomped off to continue the treasure hunt.

Nick waited until Walter was out of earshot. "You're letting him talk to you like that?" he asked Sam.

"I need an abrasive voice on the team to keep me honest. He's not wrong." She checked her watch. "We need to get a move on. There's a lot to do. The truck needs to get to the distribution hub by 6:00 a.m."

"A lot of what to do?" Nick involuntarily glanced to the location of one of the three remaining cameras above the loading bay door.

Sam followed his glance. "Walter. There's one up here." She grabbed Nick by the throat. "I'm not in much of a trusting mood anymore. Where are the rest of them?"

"Crap, Kirra. We need to head there." On the monitor Sam was pushing Nick backward with her hand tight around his throat. "Going down the gurgler pretty fast."

"You can monitor on the move?"

"I'll hotspot off my phone." He folded his laptop and stuck it under his arm. "You'll have to drive." He headed for the door. "How long will it take to get there? Not your truck."

"Not my truck. Forty-five minutes. Traffic willing."

Sam pushed Nick against the wall and held him there, her grip tight on his throat.

He held on to her wrist with his right hand, and gasped for air. "I can't breathe."

Her grip tightened a smidge. "Like I care." She flexed once then eased up. "You know how many are really here and where they are, don't you?"

"Cameras?"

She tightened her grip.

"Okay, okay. Yes. The one you saw and two more. One above the entrance door, and one in the ventilation grill on the roof, facing almost straight down. Now can you let go of my throat?"

"I should have done that much earlier. Very satisfying." Sam directed the removal of the remaining cameras.

Kirra accelerated the red convertible onto the Harbour Bridge. Davie was squeezed into the passenger seat. He had racked it all the way back and still didn't have enough leg room to comfortably use his laptop.

"You connected yet?" Kirra zipped between cars as she aimed the convertible at the M2 Motorway. She wrenched the wheel to the right to avoid colliding with a gravel truck, slamming Davie against the passenger door.

"Easy on." He adjusted himself in the seat and re-balanced the laptop on his knees. "Two cameras still connected, but there's a ladder below one of them."

"Can you see Nick?"

"Fist isn't around his throat anymore, but Sam still has him backed against a wall. Go faster."

CHAPTER THIRTY-TWO

Nick watched the one whose name he didn't know retrieve the second from last camera. "What's the deal, Sammy? How are you making enough money to pay these three apes and still come out with a bit of coin in your own pocket?"

"Punch him in the face, Sam."

"Now, now, Wally. He's got a right to know, I think," said Sam. She spread her hands out, motioning to the crates. "What do you see here?"

"Batteries. The kind used in electric vehicles. Like the company you work for. The only company in Australia currently making fully electric vehicles." He smiled. "Hey. Are you setting up your own car company to compete with Dvorak? I think you might be going about it the wrong way." He held up his hands. "But what do I know? I'm just a lowly PI."

"People always go for the complicated solution to problems that have really easy solutions." She nodded at the stacks of battery cells. "You didn't look very closely, did you?"

Walter stepped in making a slicing motion to his throat. "Sam, don't."

"He's not going to do anything about it. What can he do? You've grabbed all the cameras. He's got no proof. I'm not worried."

Walter didn't look convinced.

"Proof of what? Stealing batteries is stupid because there's no resale." He looked closer at the crates. "Three different vendors. How many vendors do Dvorak source batteries from?"

Walter looked at Sam and shook his head.

"What?" Nick craned his neck. "Wait, there's four vendors here. How many do Dvorak use?"

"Five," said Sam. She had a small smile on her face. "Used to be four."

Nick looked closer at the crates. "I only see four. Who's the fifth?"

"I am." Sam laughed at the confused look on Nick's face. "Jesus. I thought you were smart." She waved off Walter who was trying to interrupt. "Wally, you 've just scrubbed this place.."

He sneered in Nick's direction. "And for that extra work, and the lies, we'll take it out of his hide."

"Whatever chubs you, mate." Nick turned his back on Walter. "Explain this to me, Sam. How are you outsmarting everyone?"

Sam checked the time. "If you help me tonight."

"He's not helping anything. Not after this bullshit," said Walter. "I'm going to take his phone and lock him in the storage room. He'll get out when someone finds his desiccated carcass."

"Big words, mate. Can you spell them?"

Walter growled deep in his throat.

Nick nudged Sam. "I think he's pissed off. Tell me what's going on. You've got me stumped.

She waited until the final camera was turned off then took a deep breath. "Okay. Four vendors in here, right?"

"Last camera is gone. We're in the dark."

"We're still half an hour away."

"Call the police."

"And tell them what?" Kirra accelerated, passing 120 km/h.

Davie was silent. "I don't know." He closed his laptop. "Floor it."

He was pressed back in his seat as she accelerated, then she slowed, looking in the rear-view mirror.

"Shit. Police." She pulled to the shoulder of the motorway and turned off the car.

Nick re-checked the crates and nodded. "Four vendors. Why doesn't Dvorak make their own batteries? That American guy, whatshisname, makes his own."

"Why are you asking me? Not my skill set."

"Right. Stealing is."

"Stop interrupting me. I 'steal' about a thousand cases from each vendor's monthly shipment. Re-label them as coming from my company, at a very healthy profit." She looked around the warehouse. "My costs are extremely low. Especially since Dvorak is paying for these warehouses."

Nick shook his head and held up his hands. "Whoa. How many people on the inside are in on this? You'd need legal for the contracts, accounts payable to pay the bills, the auditor - " his mouth paused in an 'o' shape. "That's why you're in a hurry. The audit is coming up."

"You're close." She pushed him against the wall. "Too close."

"I'm outta here, crazy bitch." He pushed Sam back, knocking her into a stack of crates.

Walter grabbed him by the back of his shirt and threw him against the wall. "Keep your hands - hand - off of her."

Sam picked herself off the floor and dusted herself off. "Feel free to break a rib or two before you lock him in the storage room, Wally." She cleared her throat. "And make it fast. We've got a lot of work to do tonight."

Kirra held her driver's licence between her middle and index fingers, her elbow on the side the of the convertible, hand in the air.

The motorcycle cop dismounted and stood beside the car. "This your licence?"

She nodded.

He retrieved it from her fingers. "Miss Kirra Roach? This vehicle is registered to a Mr Andrew Goh." He looked across the car to Davie. "I don't suppose that's you?"

"That's not Andy. Andy is - was - my husband. He's recently deceased."

"This your new - "

"Oh, god, no." Davie squirmed in his seat. "I work for Kirra. Miss

Roach."

"I've clocked you faster than 130 km per hour." He held the breathalyser in front of Kirra's mouth. "Count to 10, slowly please."

"1 - 2 - 3 - 4 - 5 - 6 - 7 - 8 - 9 - 10." Kirra sighed. "I haven't been drinking. Can you write the ticket and let us go on our way?"

The officer handed Kirra her driver's licence. "Both of you are going to have to step out of the car. You were going more than 30 over the limit. Thirty-seven, to be precise. We're going to impound this vehicle. I can't leave you standing on the side of the road. You'll need to call someone to pick you up."

"You can't do that. We need to get to Parramatta as quickly as possible."

"The 'quickly as possible' was evident by the speed you were travelling. And this vehicle is capable of a lot more than you were doing. Out."

Davie tucked his laptop under his arm and got out of the car. "Is there someone you can call, Kirra?"

"I'm going to fight this."

"Waste of time. And we have no time to waste. Call Mike."

"I can't. The thing on his ankle."

"Anyone you explicitly, or implicitly, trust to not be involved with this?" He gently closed the car door. "Call Mike."

CHAPTER THIRTY-THREE

Walter marched Nick into the storeroom and shoved him against the wall. "You'll die in here." He hit Nick in the ribs with two hard and fast jabs and watched as Nick slumped to the floor. He bent over and pulled Nick's mobile phone from his pocket.

"No I won't," gasped Nick. "I actually have friends." He cradled his ribs. "Unlike you."

Walter followed up with a kick to the other side. "I have friends."

Nick rolled on the floor gasping for breath. "Oh, shit, that hurt."

The door slammed shut and the room went black. A very thin sliver of light leaked under the door. Nick heard the tumblers turn as Walter locked it.

"Great." He slowly rolled to his hands and knees, taking shallow breaths. "Man, this hurts."

He braced himself on the wall with his good arm and stood. Very slowly. He blinked a couple of times then forced his eyes wide open, willing his pupils to dilate as quickly as possible. He moved along the wall until he found the door and rattled the knob. It turned, but the door wouldn't move. He felt the door above the knob and found the cylinder housing for a deadbolt. "That'll do."

To the right of the door was a single light switch. He flicked it on and the naked fluorescent tube on the ceiling flickered to life.

The windowless room had empty shelving against two of the walls. A file cabinet, half its drawers open, stood in the corner. The remainder of the contents were loose paper and dust.

The shelving looked like the DIY stuff bought cheap at a hardware store. The slotted angle steel the shelves sat on would make good weapons, if he could disassemble them. The shelves were made of a pressed particle board and were jammed into place.

He knocked the underside of one of the shelves with the side of his fist, with successively harder smacks until it loosened at one end. He moved to the door and placed his ear against it. Voices, in the distance, were arguing about something.

He repeated his efforts on the other side and carefully placed the shelf against the file cabinet. Behind where the metal shelf used to be was a horizontal support piece of angled metal. A bit longer than a metre and a half. He inspected the ends where they were attached to the larger frame. Simple nut and bolt mechanism. He tested them. Too tight to loosen by hand.

Nick checked his pockets. The slot on the bolt looked like it could take a ten cent piece. The nut was square, so jamming it with the edge of the shelving should be easy.

If only he had a coin. "No weapon then. Probably for the best."

He dumped the contents of his pockets on the top of the file cabinet.

Remnants of two wireless cameras. Forty-five dollars in fives and tens. His car keys. "Not even enough to bribe my way out of here."

He picked up one of the cameras. The housing had been destroyed, but the innards looked intact. He checked the other one. Less lucky. The lens was cracked.

Davie and Kirra watched the flatbed tow truck drive off with the convertible. "This sucks."

"When is your ride arriving?" asked the officer. "It's getting dark. I can't leave you on the side of the motorway."

"Any minute now. I think your decision was unnecessary. Davie could have driven the remainder of the trip, and I can vouch for his responsibility."

"If you're ride isn't here shortly I'll have a car pick you up and take you to the nearest station."

"He'll be here."

The deep-throated rumble of an '80 muscle car down shifting interrupted them. Mike rolled to a stop on the shoulder behind the motorbike.

Kirra gave him a brief wave. "That's him. Can we go now?"

The officer slid his sunglasses on, smiled at her and put on his helmet. "Be safe."

Kirra jumped into the front seat of the car and Davie slid into the back.

"Thanks, Mike. I really appreciate it."

"How fast were you actually going?"

"A bit over 135 I think," said Davie.

Mike twisted in his seat. "You were driving?"

Kirra placed her hand on Mike's arm. "I was. Let's get going. I'll give you their address. It's a little warehouse near Parramatta."

"No, no." Mike lifted his leg. "I got this thing on. I shouldn't be here. I've got to get back to the house before the cops show." He put the car in gear.

Kirra placed her hand on his, on top of the gearshift stick. "Nick is on his own with no comms, against four people who would be more than happy to take him apart."

"You fired him. He's probably working with them now, out of spite." Realisation dawn on him. "Oh, clever. Why didn't you tell me?"

"Limiting the exposure. We've got to go there. Take us, or leave the car with us and you take an Uber back. I'll pay."

Mike hit the turn indicator, checked the traffic, and floored it. "I'll go with. I kinda liked that kid."

"Keep it to the limit. I don't need to get stopped again. Take the Windsor Road exit."

Nick was sitting on the floor, back against the locked door. He had his index and middle fingers of his right hand burrowed deep between his cast and his arm. He grunted and raised his left elbow in the air and shook his arm. "I think…" He pushed his hand as far and as hard as he could into the cast. His finger just grasped the thin case of tools. The tenuous grip required slow and gentle extraction until he could grab it firmly and pull it out. "…I've got it."

He slid open the thin zipper along the edge and opened the case like a book. Three lock pick tools on each side.

He smiled.

He eased to his feet, holding his ribs and inspected the deadbolt lock. It was cheap. A torsion key and a rake would do it in seconds.

Nick took a deep breath and picked the working camera off the file cabinet. He slid the recessed switch to the on position, gave it a second to sync, then held it at arm's length in front of his face. "Hey Davie, I can't tell if you're seeing this or not, but I'm still at the warehouse near Parramatta. Get cops. Sam's running some kind of scam with Dvorak. She's got someone, or ones, inside the company helping her. I'm going to try getting out of here, but I'll stick this somewhere before I leave. If I can."

He stuck the camera in his pocket and applied torsion to the deadbolt lock. He used a simple rake and scrubbed the pins while applying torsion. Twelve seconds after he started, the torsion bar gave and the deadbolt retracted. He pocketed the lock pick set.

He turned the doorknob and squatted as he eased open the door. He had a clear view to the loading dock on his left. All four of them were there. Sam and Walter were loading the truck while the other two were prising open crates, and relabelling the crates and their contents with Sam's phony battery company name.

He checked the distance to the main door to the right. Uninjured he could probably make it in ten fast seconds. With a broken arm and at least three untreated fractured ribs, more like 20 to 30 seconds. Plus, he wanted to stick the camera somewhere.

Walter turned off the main road in Parramatta and his headlights played across a row of old warehouses. "Around here somewhere?"

Davie leaned between the front seats and pointed to the right. "Down that cul-de-sac. Third warehouse on the right. Roll in quietly. If they've got their hands on Nick we don't want to spook them." Davie sat back and opened his laptop.

"What are you doing?" asked Kirra.

"Hoping."

Nick eased out of the storage room and quietly closed the door behind him. There was a small ledge above the door frame. The four at the loading bay still had their backs to him. He reached up and carefully placed the camera on the door jamb facing the loading bay.

He backed away slowly, trying to be as quiet his battered body could be, easing his way to the front door, and banged into a metal bucket and mop, sending them clattering across the floor.

The four at the loading bay stopped their work and turned.

Nick swallowed. "Oh shit."

CHAPTER THIRTY-FOUR

Davie opened the video monitoring software and checked the first bank of cameras for this location. All black. "Damn." He checked the second bank. Five of the six squares were black, but the sixth square had a slightly askew view of the loading dock. Sam and her three lug heads were turned away from the truck they appeared to have been loading and were staring just past the camera.

"Pull over. Quick."

Mike hauled the car to the kerb. "What?"

"Nick seems to have gotten a camera back online. And based on the images I'm seeing, he's running away from them toward the front door."

"Then why did we stop?" Mike gunned the car into the warehouse parking lot and up to the office door. There were no external lights. The lot was illuminated by sparsely space streetlights.

"Next warehouse, mate. You've pulled up short."

Mike grumbled something under his breath and floored the

accelerator as he yanked the wheel to the right. He left rubber on the parking lot as he bounced out of the driveway, onto the street, and into the next driveway. He reached the door just as it flew open and Nick was propelled onto the stairs. A large man was right behind him, gaining quickly. Sam brought up the rear.

Mike stopped jumped to the front of the car. "Need a hand, Nick?"

"Got a cricket bat?"

Mike chuckled. "I think we'll be fine without. Are you getting out, Davie?"

Davie slowly exited the car. Kirra was by the front fender. Nick reached the front of the car as Sam and her friends reached the bottom of the metal stairs.

"Sam. What's going on?" asked Kirra.

Walter stepped in front of her. "Who the hell are you?"

"She runs Dvorak, you moron." Sam pushed him out of the way. "Why are you here?"

Kirra shook her head. "You were my favourite. How much have you stolen from me?"

"Yeah, I don't know what you're talking about."

"It's all recorded, Sam," said Nick. "Every bit of it."

Sam stood a bit straighter. "I really don't know what you're talking about."

"Let us have a look at what's inside," said Kirra. "I am paying for this place."

Sam frowned. "No. Walter and I are starting up an indoor paintball facility. The lease is in my company name. We expect to be up and running in about three months. It's empty in there right now. I've got a lot of shopping to do." She jammed her hands in her pockets and thrust her chin forward. "To my original question, what are you doing here?"

Kirra pushed forward. "I'm checking out the interior."

Walter stepped in front of her with his hands up. "I normally don't hit women, but I'm about to make an exception."

"Watch it, mate." Mike stepped up beside Kirra. "You're not that big."

Davie stood beside Mike.

Nick looked at Walter and Sam. Shook his head. "Something feels off. Where are the other two?"

He took the laptop and checked the videos. "Hey, these two are stalling. The other two are shoving crates into the truck out back."

"Outta my way." Mike shoved Walter in the chest, staggering him back. "I'll drop you, hard." He shoved again but Walter stepped out of the way and Mike stumbled. Walter caught him on the side of the head with a looping roundhouse, helping Mike on the way to the pavement and cracking a couple of bones in Walter's hand.

"Son of a bitch." He cradled his hand and hopped away.

Kirra pushed Sam out of the way. "Move, princess."

Sam lunged for Kirra and Nick jumped up to grab her arm. "Enough, Sam. I've got enough to put you away."

She wrenched free and kicked Nick on the side of the leg. He buckled and swore. "Davie. Don't just stand there."

Kirra reached the top of the steps and was reaching for the door when Sam caught up to her.

"Leave it."

Kirra pushed Sam against the railing and pinned her. "You're trying to destroy my company. No way in hell I'm going to 'leave it'. Tell me what 'it' was."

Davie ducked past them and opened the door. Nick limped in after him. The warehouse was almost completely empty. The truck, on the other hand, was three quarters full. And getting fuller as the other two of the quartet continued to load it. It sat heavy.

"Where'd you put the camera?" asked Davie.

Nick pointed to the top of the storeroom door. "What are we doing in here? One and a half of us."

Davie shrugged. "I'm winging it, mate. Not too happy about it, but here we are." He cleared his throat. "Let's go get them." He grabbed the camera off the top of the door jamb as he passed it and handed it to Nick.

Walter looked up from his rapidly bruising, and swelling, hand. "Jesus, that hurts." He watched Mike slowly get to his feet. "What in the hell is your head made of, mate? Ironbark?"

Mike stood and rolled his shoulders. "Stay away from her."

Walter held up his hands. "My final payment comes through tomorrow. I've nothing left to do with any of this." He looked at the bruising blooming on the back of his hand. "Barely worth it." He pulled his helmet off the back of his bike. "Hope to never see you again."

"Where you think you're going?" Mike stood in front of the bike, blocking Walter's exit.

"None of your business. Out of my way."

The remaining two thieves in the warehouse stepped up their pace moving crates. It was heavy work, so the pace wasn't stepped up that much.

"Jesus, I want a bigger cut. Where are Sam and Walter?" They bent over to manoeuvre another crate onto the handcart.

"Skipped out on you two," said Davie.

They slowly stood and turned to face Davie and Nick.

"You aren't as smart as you think you are, if you think coming back in here was smart."

Davie frowned and looked at Nick. "Do you understand what this chump is trying to say?"

"Nope." Nick limped over to the truck. "You didn't finish the labelling. Why are you wasting your time? This is done."

Mike ran in behind them. "Need any help, guys?"

'I think we've got this, mate. How's your head?"

Mike looked at the one-armed Nick and overweight Davie and chuckled. "Okay. Have at it. I'll be here if you need me." He stepped sideways out of the way and hit the crowbar with his foot. He glanced at it, then looked closer. "Oh, this is good."

Barry looked at Alan. Shook his head. "I'm not getting hung for this." He jumped off the loading dock and headed to his bike.

Alan dropped his end of the crate. "Screw it. This isn't worth it." He turned to jump off the loading dock when he saw the reflection of red and blue lights. "Ah, shit." He turned and ran to the front of the warehouse and was stopped at the door by the policeman entering.

CHAPTER THIRTY-FIVE

Nick limped down the front steps. There were three police cars parked around Mike's car, lights flashing. Sam and Walter were in cuffs. Kirra was talking quietly with Sam. Nick started limping toward them when he noticed that Mike was in cuffs also, seated on the ground with his back against his car.

Nick buttonholed one of the uniforms. "Hey, that guy is one of the good guys. He shouldn't be cuffed."

Mike lifted his foot. His trouser slipped up his leg exposing his monitoring bracelet. "It's okay, Nick. How do you think the cops got here so fast?"

"Yeah, well, he's only here because I was in trouble. You should cut him loose."

"Not my decision, son."

Nick shook his head and limped over to Sam and Kirra. "Was it worth it?"

"Piss off."

"Who killed Andy?"

Sam swallowed. "That was Walter."

Walter struggled against his cuffs. "Shut up, you bitch. You were as involved as I was."

"No, no. I watched him do it. I should have reported it at the time, but…" She trailed off.

"We'll add accessory after the fact, then," said the officer. "Let's go." She took Sam by the arm.

"Can you give me a minute?" ask Kirra. "I'd really appreciate it. Only a minute. Thanks, Sandy."

"No problem, Kir."

Nick leaned close to Kirra. "You know her?"

"School friend." Kirra leaned toward Sam. "Who was working with you on the inside?"

"Nobody."

"Bullshit, Sam. I'll find them. You help and maybe they'll go easy on you."

"Who needs someone on the inside? I've got almost total access to all of the systems. Trusted IT professional, right? Not immune to audits, but all of the incriminating stuff will be deleted well before the internal auditor starts their work."

Kirra took out her phone and stepped away. "Siri, call Brent." She glanced at Sam and walked out of earshot.

Nick leaned against the car. Took the mini-camera out of his pocket and held it loosely, concealed in his hand "What did you hit Andy with? We couldn't find a weapon."

"I found it," yelled Mike from the ground. "One of you uniforms go grab the crowbar from the warehouse. Ten bucks says it was used to bash in Andy's head." He glanced at Kirra. "Sorry, boss."

"Walter kept the crowbar? Jesus, what an idiot." Sam ignored the protests coming from inside the police car. "I didn't think we needed to do it."

An unmarked car rolled into the parking lot, red and blue lights flashing in the grill. Wallace and Lin exited and headed directly toward Nick and Mike.

Wallace tapped Nick on the arm. "You and your nose."

"Doing your job. Sam arranged for Andy's death. Got her friend Walter," Nick pointed at the police car, "to pummel him. I was just sussing out what the murder weapon was."

"The crowbar," yelled Mike. "It's in the warehouse, for shits sake."

"I didn't arrange it," protested Sam. "It wasn't my idea."

"BULLSHIT." Walter's roar could be heard through the closed cop car windows.

Wallace motioned for a uniform to take Sam. "Put her in a different car than her friend." He leaned on the car Walter was in and opened the back door. "What's your name?"

"Piss off, copper."

"Your parents must not love you. It was Sam's idea to kill Andy?"

"I want a deal."

"I don't think you have anything to deal with."

"Sam told me she'd pay me an extra 100 grand if I got rid of Andy. That enough?"

Wallace smiled, stepped back and closed the door. "Idiot. Don't need to deal now." He moved to the car holding Sam. Opened the door. "You paid him an extra 250k to knock off Andy?"

"No way. It was a hundo." She closed her eyes. "Shit."

"A whole gang of idiots." Wallace closed the door and motioned for Mike to stand up. He removed the cuffs and bent down and removed the monitoring bracelet. "Don't need these anymore. Someone is going to need to explain to me what we're doing here." He nodded at Mike. "Other than the unnecessary apprehension of an out of place ankle monitor."

Kirra finished her call. "It was pretty clever."

"That surprises me."

"Sam has wormed her way into our contracts and accounts payable systems to rip me off for about 6 million a month. Give or take. Depends on the volumes of cars we produce." She scratched the back of her head. "It's difficult to explain."

"I think I figured it out." Nick leaned against the car, supporting his damaged knee. "She'd skim 1000 units from each of the four battery vendors. She increased the per unit amount to correspond with the decreased number of units so the total contract value didn't change. Kept the vendors in the dark. She did that to the four existing vendors.

"Then she created a dummy fifth vendor. Created fake contracts for that vendor for the 4000 units per month." He pointed at the warehouse. "She had to have someone helping in the distribution center - "

"That's where Walter worked, Nick."

"Thanks, Kirra. Walter would arrange for the physical skimming of a thousand units per vendor before they were officially received and have them shipped here. This is where the units were relabelled and re-crated to whatever Sam's dummy company was. Then she'd send them back to the distribution centre, have them officially received, and invoice the company. $1500 a battery, that's $6 million a month. For eleven months. This would have been the twelfth, and last. Seventy-two million dollars, all up."

Lin nodded. "Clever. Wouldn't pass an audit, though."

Kirra was repeatedly clenching her jaw muscles, glaring furiously at Sam. "Our internal auditors start work in a week and a half. They'd definitely catch the discrepancies between the online contracts and the original paper copies. Also, the fact there was a dummy corporation setup sending payments to an unauthorised bank account. Sam had a script in place to reverse everything at the end of the week. Emphasis on 'had'. My CFO is going to get our IT team find it and disable it. I'll let the auditors know what happened and let them dig up all the evidence." She smiled. "Debating whether I tell them ahead of time or let them freak out when they find it."

"Well," said Wallace. "That looks to be that. If the four of you can come into the station sometime in the next couple of days and give me your official statements, that would be great." He turned to his partner with his hand out.

"What?" asked Lin.

Wallace smiled.

She scowled as she took out her wallet and gave him $50. "Don't be smug."

"Can I ask a favour, Detective?" asked Kirra.

"Sure." He tucked the $50 into his wallet and stowed it in his inside suit pocket "Whether I can grant it or not depends on how big it is."

Kirra smiled embarrassedly. "I, um, was heading out here with Dave - Davie - in my car when I was pulled over for speeding. Kinda fast."

"I'm not going to fix tickets. Couldn't even if I wanted to."

"Oh, I don't mind if I get a ticket. Don't even mind if my licence is suspended. But the car was impounded. It was my husband's. I'd really like to get it back."

Wallace looked at Lin. "I think we can do that." They turned and got in their car and left.

Kirra and Davie and Mike and Nick watched the patrol cars depart until the reflections from the blue and red lights were no longer visible.

"Well." Nick pushed himself off Mike's car. "Can someone take me to the hospital? I think my knee is fucked."

CHAPTER THIRTY-SIX

Nick leaned his crutch against the wall and eased into the chair at the desk in his study. He smiled. His study. Only a few months ago his study was a tattered sofa in front of a shit TV. Now he was living in the guest house at Kirra's place. For a time. He had a few places to look at, but she agreed he could wait until his knee was good again.

His leg was in a brace. Torn ACL. Six weeks in a brace -- five more to go -- and another six weeks of physiotherapy and he'd be as good as new. Better, he'd been told, since his exercise regime prior to the injury was almost non-existent. And the physio assured him the rehab would be brutal.

He picked a ruler off the desk and slid it between the cast and his arm. The knee injury was preferable to this. He angled the ruler in an attempt to quell the itching. Another four and a half weeks of this and he was going to be certifiable.

"You shouldn't do that. It only makes it worse."

Nick slowly spun in his chair, carefully making sure his extended leg didn't bounce off anything fixed. "Kirra! Hey, how's it going? I thought you were heading to New York."

"That's tomorrow evening. How are things progressing?"

Nick grimaced. "The bank accounts were frozen, the ones Dvorak was sending money to for the battery cell scam, but she'd already transferred most of it out to overseas accounts. It's unlikely more than a couple of million will be recovered, and most of that from her accomplices."

Kirra sat. She finger combed her hair back. "Overseas accounts?"

Nick nodded. "I tracked most of the transfers to Isle of Man. Great place if you want to avoid taxes, but not the best from a secrecy point of view. I believe that was just the first step, after which she converted it to digital currency, like Bitcoin. It'll be near impossible to trace after that." He grunted. "Even though I think digital currency is this century's tulip craze."

Kirra waved away his concerns. "The company will survive. But I'll give you 10% of whatever you can recover. Enough incentive?"

"I - don't know."

"You want more?" She laughed. "I didn't expect that."

"Oh, no, god, no. I don't know if I'll be able to recover *any* of it. A lot of work for no pay." He shrugged. "Any better offers?"

She chuckled and stood. "Just set up the new financial governance framework. I'm paying you well enough for that. I don't want it possible for anything like this to happen again." She cleared her throat. "But enough work for you today. I'm going out on the boat. I'd like you and Davie to join us."

Davie rubbed a thick layer of sunscreen on his face and neck.

Nick laughed. "Don't forget your ears, mate."

They were standing with Cameron on the jetty, beside the 15m catamaran. "Yeah, don't worry. I'm good at this. I'm mostly English and Scot. I burn at the sight of a glass of orange juice."

"That makes no sense." Nick held the bottle of sunscreen while Davie went to work on his face.

"What's this about?"

"We'll find out soon enough."

"Are you joining us, Cam?"

"No. I've got things to do here."

Mike poked his head up from below decks. "You two twats going to stand there all day?" He popped back below deck for a second, then popped back up with a couple of life jackets. "Wear these."

He tossed them on the deck climbed up to the helm. "Kirra's below deck. We leave in a couple of minutes."

"To where?" asked Nick.

"Put those things on." He looked over his shoulder at the stern of the boat. "Cameron. Untie us, would you?"

It was a perfect day to be on the water. Not a cloud in the sky, with a light southerly breeze keeping the sun's heat to a bearable level. Nick and Davie sat either end of a large bench seat on the upper deck of the boat near the stern.

Kirra came above deck with a tray of drinks. "Guys, you don't need those life jackets. It's almost dead calm, we're using engines and this is a big, stable boat. It's not going over.

Davie took off his floatation vest and dropped it on the seat beside him. "Maybe I don't, but my boy here can't swim for shit. Best he keeps his on."

"What he said. Especially with my knee. And my arm." Nick took one of the glasses of beer. "Thanks. Where are we going?"

"Andy's favourite surf spot."

Nick nodded. "Oh. Okay." He sipped the beer. "I don't know what to say."

"Nothing for you to say. Enjoy the ride. It's a beautiful day." She handed the other beer to Davie and walked out to the bow of the catamaran and sat on the deck, holding onto the railing.

"What's that about?"

"Just enjoy the ride, mate."

Mike piloted the catamaran north-east past Hornby Lighthouse on their right, then turned east to leave the harbour. Once they cleared North Head he headed north until they were off Manly Beach.

Mike stopped the engine when they were about 200 m offshore, facing the beach.

"What's this?" Davie placed his glass in the depression on the table in front of them and stood. "What's going on up front?"

Nick reached out and stopped him. "Andy's favourite surf spot. Kirra's spreading his ashes." He stood and watched as Mike walked up to join her and handed her the urn.

A breeze blew toward them from the coast. "It's going to blow in her face," said Davie. "We should warn them."

The wind stopped dead.

"Maybe not." Nick smiled.

Kirra and Mike stood beside each other, heads bowed, and after a couple of seconds Kirra opened the urn, handed the top to Mike, and slowly poured the ashes into the ocean. She wiped tears from her eyes, put the top back on the urn and returned to the stern.

"Thanks for coming with us. Andy would really appreciate what you've done."

"It's an honour, Kirra. Are you okay?"

She smiled. "I am. Thanks. Mike's cooking up some food in the galley. Dinner will be ready shortly. It'd be a shame to waste a day like this."

Davie watched her as she walked away. "So, she's single …"

Nick laughed. "Not in the same league. Not even close." He changed the subject. "How's the systems work going?"

'Trivial. Emailed it to you before we left. I've been working on the Bitcoin thing. I think I can track it down."

"How? Never mind. I wouldn't understand. Chance of recovery?"

Davie waggled his hand. "Probably more than half."

"Huh." He smiled. "I'll give you 5 percent of anything you recover."

"You can do that?"

"I can do that."

"You've got a deal."

<<<>>>

About the Author

Tony McFadden is a displaced Canadian now calling Australia his home. He and his wife and two children live near the beaches where he spends as much of his time as possible writing.

More about Tony and his writing can be found on the interwebs at TonyMcFadden.net/mybooks, Facebook and Twitter.

Also by Tony McFadden

G'Day LA • G'Day USA

Matt's War • Daly Battles: The Fall of Pyongyang • Target: Australia

Book 'Em - An Eamonn Shute Mystery • Unprotected Sax • Family Matters

Have Wormhole, Will Travel • Killing Time

Mac D: Private Investigator • A Step Too Far (A Mac D Case) • Hunter/Prey (A Mac D Case)

The Murder of Jeremy Brookes (A McGinnis Investigations Case) • Number Fifteen (A McGinnis Investigations Case)

And up next...

Blue Mountain High

Nick Harding has a new case. Two of them.

A very rich old dude is about to kick off and is desperate to make amends with his estranged son. And leave him a heap of cash. Nick is contacted by the old guy's lawyer with a task: Find the son, convince him to get in contact with his father, and help mediate the relationship. Nick hates mediating.

At nearly the same time, a friend of a friend engages him to track down a serial deadbeat who has bilked a small finance company out of a lot of their money. The fee is lower, but the job is more up Nick's alley.

Then the heir's life is threatened, the deadbeat has a compelling backstory and everything Nick thought he knew was wrong.

Coming in early 2022.